NON SANZ DROICT.

William Shakespeare

THE SONNETS

With New Literary Criticism
and an Updated Bibliography

INTRODUCTION BY W. H. AUDEN

EDITED BY WILLIAM BURTO

THE SIGNET CLASSIC SHAKESPEARE
GENERAL EDITOR: SYLVAN BARNET

A SIGNET CLASSIC

SIGNET CLASSIC
Published by the Penguin Group
Penguin Books USA Inc., 375 Hudson Street,
New York, New York 10014, U.S.A.
Penguin Books Ltd, 27 Wrights Lane,
London W8 5TZ, England
Penguin Books Australia Ltd, Ringwood,
Victoria, Australia
Penguin Books Canada Ltd, 10 Alcorn Avenue,
Toronto, Ontario, Canada M4V 3B2
Penguin Books (N.Z.) Ltd, 182–190 Wairau Road,
Auckland 10, New Zealand

Penguin Books Ltd, Registered Offices:
Harmondsworth, Middlesex, England

23   22   21   20   19   18   17   16

 REGISTERED TRADEMARK—MARCA REGISTRADA

Library of Congress Catalog Card Number: 88-61101

Printed in the United States of America

Contents

Shakespeare: Prefatory Remarks

Between the record of his baptism in Stratford on 26 April 1564 and the record of his burial in Stratford on 25 April 1616, some forty documents name Shakespeare, and many others name his parents, his children, and his grandchildren. More facts are known about William Shakespeare than about any other playwright of the period except Ben Jonson. The facts should, however, be distinguished from the legends. The latter, inevitably more engaging and better known, tell us that the Stratford boy killed a calf in high style, poached deer and rabbits, and was forced to flee to London, where he held horses outside a playhouse. These traditions are only traditions; they may be true, but no evidence supports them, and it is well to stick to the facts.

Mary Arden, the dramatist's mother, was the daughter of a substantial landowner; about 1557 she married John Shakespeare, who was a glove-maker and trader in various farm commodities. In 1557 John Shakespeare was a member of the Council (the governing body of Stratford), in 1558 a constable of the borough, in 1561 one of the two town chamberlains, in 1565 an alderman (entitling him to the appellation "Mr."), in 1568 high bailiff—the town's highest political office, equivalent to mayor. After 1577, for an unknown reason he drops out of local politics. The birthday of William Shakespeare, the eldest son of this locally prominent man, is unrecorded; but the Stratford parish register records that the infant was baptized on 26 April 1564. (It is quite possible that he was born on 23 April, but this date has probably been assigned by tradition because it is the date on which, fifty-two years later, he died.) The at-

tendance records of the Stratford grammar school of the
period are not extant, but it is reasonable to assume that the
son of a local official attended the school and received sub-
stantial training in Latin. The masters of the school from
Shakespeare's seventh to fifteenth years held Oxford de-
grees; the Elizabethan curriculum excluded mathematics
and the natural sciences but taught a good deal of Latin
rhetoric, logic, and literature. On 27 November 1582 a mar-
riage license was issued to Shakespeare and Anne Hathaway,
eight years his senior. The couple had a child in May, 1583.
Perhaps the marriage was necessary, but perhaps the couple
had earlier engaged in a formal "troth plight" which would
render their children legitimate even if no further ceremony
were performed. In 1585 Ann Hathaway bore Shakespeare
twins.

That Shakespeare was born is excellent; that he married
and had children is pleasant; but that we know nothing
about his departure from Stratford to London, or about
the beginning of his theatrical career, is lamentable and
must be admitted. We would gladly sacrifice details about
his children's baptism for details about his earliest days on
the stage. Perhaps the poaching episode is true (but it is first
reported almost a century after Shakespeare's death), or
perhaps he first left Stratford to be a schoolteacher, as
another tradition holds; perhaps he was moved by

> Such wind as scatters young men through the world,
> To seek their fortunes further than at home
> Where small experience grows.

In 1592, thanks to the cantankerousness of Robert
Greene, a rival playwright and a pamphleteer, we have our
first reference, a snarling one, to Shakespeare as an actor
and playwright. Greene warns those of his own educated
friends who wrote for the theater against an actor who has
presumed to turn playwright:

> There is an upstart crow, beautified with our feathers, that
> with his *tiger's heart wrapped in a player's hide* supposes
> he is as well able to bombast out a blank verse as the best

of you, and being an absolute Johannes-factotum is in his
own conceit the only Shake-scene in a country.

The reference to the player, as well as the allusion to
Aesop's crow (who strutted in borrowed plumage, as an
actor struts in fine words not his own), makes it clear that
by this date Shakespeare had both acted and written. That
Shakespeare is meant is indicated not only by "Shake-scene"
but by the parody of a line from one of Shakespeare's plays,
3 Henry VI: "O, tiger's heart wrapped in a woman's hide."
If Shakespeare in 1592 was prominent enough to be at-
tacked by an envious dramatist, he probably had served an
apprenticeship in the theater for at least a few years.

In any case, by 1592 Shakespeare had acted and written,
and there are a number of subsequent references to him as
an actor: documents indicate that in 1598 he is a "principal
comedian," in 1603 a "principal tragedian," in 1608 he is
one of the "men players." The profession of actor was not
for a gentleman, and it occasionally drew the scorn of
university men who resented writing speeches for persons
less educated than themselves, but it was respectable
enough: players, if prosperous, were in effect members of
the bourgeoisie, and there is nothing to suggest that Strat-
ford considered William Shakespeare less than a solid citi-
zen. When, in 1596, the Shakespeares were granted a coat
of arms, the grant was made to Shakespeare's father, but
probably William Shakespeare (who the next year bought
the second-largest house in town) had arranged the matter
on his own behalf. In subsequent transactions he is occa-
sionally styled a gentleman.

Although in 1593 and 1594 Shakespeare published two
narrative poems dedicated to the Earl of Southampton,
Venus and Adonis and *The Rape of Lucrece,* and may well
have written most or all of his sonnets in the middle nineties,
Shakespeare's literary activity seems to have been almost
entirely devoted to the theater. (It may be significant that
the two narrative poems were written in years when the
plague closed the theaters for several months.) In 1594 he
was a charter member of a theatrical company called the
Chamberlain's Men (which in 1603 changed its name to the

King's Men); until he retired to Stratford (about 1611, apparently), he was with this remarkably stable company. From 1599 the company acted primarily at the Globe Theatre, in which Shakespeare held a one-tenth interest. Other Elizabethan dramatists are known to have acted, but no other is known also to have been entitled to a share in the profits of the playhouse.

Shakespeare's first eight published plays did not have his name on them, but this is not remarkable; the most popular play of the sixteenth century, Thomas Kyd's *The Spanish Tragedy,* went through many editions without naming Kyd, and Kyd's authorship is known only because a book on the profession of acting happens to quote (and attribute to Kyd) some lines on the interest of Roman emperors in the drama. What is remarkable is that after 1598 Shakespeare's name commonly appears on printed plays—some of which are not his. Another indication of his popularity comes from Francis Meres, author of *Palladis Tamia: Wit's Treasury* (1598): in this anthology of snippets accompanied by an essay on literature, many playwrights are mentioned, but Shakespeare's name occurs more often than any other, and Shakespeare is the only playwright whose plays are listed.

From his acting, playwriting, and share in a theater, Shakespeare seems to have made considerable money. He put it to work, making substantial investments in Stratford real estate. When he made his will (less than a month before he died), he sought to leave his property intact to his descendants. Of small bequests to relatives and to friends (including three actors, Richard Burbage, John Heminges, and Henry Condell), that to his wife of the second-best bed has provoked the most comment; perhaps it was the bed the couple had slept in, the best being reserved for visitors. In any case, had Shakespeare not excepted it, the bed would have gone (with the rest of his household possessions) to his daughter and her husband. On 25 April 1616 he was buried within the chancel of the church at Stratford. An unattractive monument to his memory, placed on a wall near the grave, says he died on 23 April. Over the grave itself are the lines, perhaps by Shakespeare, that (more than his literary fame) have kept his bones

undisturbed in the crowded burial ground where old bones
were often dislodged to make way for new:

> Good friend, for Jesus' sake forbear
> To dig the dust enclosèd here.
> Blessed be the man that spares these stones
> And cursed be he that moves my bones.

Thirty-seven plays, as well as some nondramatic poems,
are held to constitute the Shakespeare canon. The dates
of composition of most of the works are highly uncertain,
but there is often evidence of a *terminus a quo* (starting
point) and/or a *terminus ad quem* (terminal point) that
provides a framework for intelligent guessing. For ex-
ample, *Richard II* cannot be earlier than 1595, the pub-
lication date of some material to which it is indebted; *The
Merchant of Venice* cannot be later than 1598, the year
Francis Meres mentioned it. Sometimes arguments for a
date hang on an alleged topical allusion, such as the lines
about the unseasonable weather in *A Midsummer Night's
Dream,* II.i.81–117, but such an allusion (if indeed it is an
allusion) can be variously interpreted, and in any case
there is always the possibility that a topical allusion was
inserted during a revision, years after the composition of
a play. Dates are often attributed on the basis of style,
and although conjectures about style usually rest on other
conjectures, sooner or later one must rely on one's literary
sense. There is no real proof, for example, that *Othello*
is not as early as *Romeo and Juliet,* but one feels *Othello*
is later, and because the first record of its performance is
1604, one is glad enough to set its composition at that
date and not push it back into Shakespeare's early years.
The following chronology, then, is as much indebted to
informed guesswork and sensitivity as it is to fact. The
dates, necessarily imprecise, indicate something like a
scholarly consensus.

PLAYS

1588–93	*The Comedy of Errors*
1588–94	*Love's Labor's Lost*
1590–91	*2 Henry VI*
1590–91	*3 Henry VI*
1591–92	*1 Henry VI*
1592–93	*Richard III*
1592–94	*Titus Andronicus*
1593–94	*The Taming of the Shrew*
1593–95	*The Two Gentlemen of Verona*
1594–96	*Romeo and Juliet*
1595	*Richard II*
1594–96	*A Midsummer Night's Dream*
1596–97	*King John*
1596–97	*The Merchant of Venice*
1597	*1 Henry IV*
1597–98	*2 Henry IV*
1598–1600	*Much Ado About Nothing*
1598–99	*Henry V*
1599	*Julius Caesar*
1599–1600	*As You Like It*
1599–1600	*Twelfth Night*
1600–01	*Hamlet*
1597–1601	*The Merry Wives of Windsor*
1601–02	*Troilus and Cressida*
1602–04	*All's Well That Ends Well*
1603–04	*Othello*
1604	*Measure for Measure*
1605–06	*King Lear*
1605–06	*Macbeth*
1606–07	*Antony and Cleopatra*
1605–08	*Timon of Athens*
1607–09	*Coriolanus*
1608–09	*Pericles*
1609–10	*Cymbeline*
1610–11	*The Winter's Tale*
1611	*The Tempest*
1612–13	*Henry VIII*

POEMS

1592	*Venus and Adonis*
1593–94	*The Rape of Lucrece*
1593–1600	*Sonnets*
1600–01	*The Phoenix and the Turtle*

The Texts of Shakespeare

Though eighteen of his plays were published during his lifetime, Shakespeare seems never to have supervised their publication. There is nothing unusual here; when a playwright sold a play to a theatrical company he surrendered his ownership of it. Normally a company would not publish the play, because to publish it meant to allow competitors to acquire the piece. Some plays, however, did get published: apparently treacherous actors sometimes pieced together a play for a publisher, sometimes a company in need of money sold a play, and sometimes a company allowed a play to be published that no longer drew audiences. That Shakespeare did not concern himself with publication, then, is scarcely remarkable; of his contemporaries only Ben Jonson carefully supervised the publication of his own plays. In 1623, seven years after Shakespeare's death, John Heminges and Henry Condell (two senior members of Shakespeare's company, who had performed with him for about twenty years) collected his plays—published and unpublished—into a large volume, commonly called the First Folio. (A folio is a volume consisting of sheets that have been folded once, each sheet thus making two leaves, or four pages. The eighteen plays published during Shakespeare's lifetime had been issued one play per volume in small books called quartos. Each sheet in a quarto has been folded twice, making four leaves, or eight pages.) The First Folio contains thirty-six plays; a thirty-seventh, *Pericles,* though not in the Folio, is regarded as canonical, as are the sonnets and the narrative poems. Heminges and Condell suggest in an address "To the great variety of readers" that the republished plays are presented in better form than in the quartos: "Before you were abused with diverse stolen and surreptitious copies, maimed and deformed by the frauds and stealths of injurious impostors that exposed them; even those, are now offered to your view cured and perfect of their limbs, and all the rest absolute in their numbers, as he [i.e., Shakespeare] conceived them."

Whoever was assigned to prepare the texts for publication in the First Folio seems to have taken his job seriously and yet not to have performed it with uniform care. The sources of the texts seem to have been, in general, good unpublished copies or the best published copies. The first play in the collection, *The Tempest*, is divided into acts and scenes, has unusually full stage directions and descriptions of spectacle, and concludes with a list of the characters, but the editor was not able (or willing) to present all of the succeeding texts so fully dressed. Later texts occasionally show signs of carelessness: in one scene of *Much Ado About Nothing* the names of actors, instead of characters, appear as speech prefixes, as they had in the quarto, which the Folio reprints; proofreading throughout the Folio is spotty and apparently was done without reference to the printer's copy; the pagination of *Hamlet* jumps from 156 to 257.

A modern editor of Shakespeare must first select his copy; no problem if the play exists only in the Folio, but a considerable problem if the relationship between a quarto and the Folio—or an early quarto and a later one—is unclear. When an editor has chosen what seems to him to be the most authoritative text or texts for his copy, he has not done with making decisions. First of all, he must reckon with Elizabethan spelling. If he is not producing a facsimile, he probably modernizes it, but ought he to preserve the old form of words that apparently were pronounced quite unlike their modern forms—"lanthorn" "alablaster"? If he preserves these forms, is he really preserving Shakespeare's forms or perhaps those of a compositor in the printing house? What is one to do when one finds "lanthorn" and "lantern" in adjacent lines? (The editors of this series in general, but not invariably, assume

that words should be spelled in their modern form.) Eliza-
bethan punctuation, too, presents problems. For example
in the First Folio, the only text for the play, Macbeth re-
jects his wife's idea that he can wash the blood from his
hand:

> no: this my Hand will rather
> The multitudinous Seas incarnardine,
> Making the Greene one, Red.

Obviously an editor will remove the superfluous capitals,
and he will probably alter the spelling to "incarnadine,"
but will he leave the comma before "red," letting Macbeth
speak of the sea as "the green one," or will he (like most
modern editors) remove the comma and thus have Mac-
beth say that his hand will make the ocean *uniformly* red?
    An editor will sometimes have to change more than
spelling or punctuation. Macbeth says to his wife:

> I dare do all that may become a man,
> Who dares no more, is none.

For two centuries editors have agreed that the second line
is unsatisfactory, and have emended "no" to "do": "Who
dares do more is none." Similarly, editors are agreed that
in the twenty-fifth sonnet something needs to be emended.
Line 9 reads: "The painefull warrier famosed for worth,"
but line 11, with which it should rhyme, reads: "Is from
the booke of honour rased quite." One can alter "worth"
to "fight" or to "might," or one can retain "worth" and
alter "quite" to "forth." Where necessary such changes
have been made, but the editors of the Signet Classic Shake-
speare have restrained themselves from making abundant
emendations. In their minds they hear Dr. Johnson on the
dangers of emending: "I have adopted the Roman senti-
ment, that it is more honorable to save a citizen than to
kill an enemy." Some departures (in addition to spelling,
punctuation, and lineation) from the copy text have of
course been made, but the original readings are listed in
a note following the play, so that the reader can evaluate
them for himself.

No editor during the course of his work can fail to recollect some words Heminges and Condell prefixed to the Folio:

> It had been a thing, we confess, worthy to have been wished, that the author himself had lived to have set forth and overseen his own writings. But since it hath been ordained otherwise, and he by death departed from that right, we pray you do not envy his friends the office of their care and pain to have collected and published them.

Nor can an editor, after he has done his best, forget Heminges and Condell's final words: "And so we leave you to other of his friends, whom if you need can be your guides. If you need them not, you can lead yourselves, and others. And such readers we wish him."

SYLVAN BARNET
Tufts University

Introduction

Probably, more nonsense has been talked and written, more intellectual and emotional energy expended in vain, on the sonnets of Shakespeare than on any other literary work in the world. Indeed, they have become the best touchstone I know of for distinguishing the sheep from the goats, those, that is, who love poetry for its own sake and understand its nature, from those who only value poems either as historical documents or because they express feelings or beliefs of which the reader happens to approve.

It so happens that we know almost nothing about the historical circumstances under which Shakespeare wrote these sonnets: we don't know to whom they are addressed or exactly when they were written, and, unless entirely new evidence should turn up, which is unlikely, we never shall.

This has not prevented many very learned gentlemen from displaying their scholarship and ingenuity in conjecture. Though it seems to me rather silly to spend much time upon conjectures which cannot be proved true or false, that is not my real objection to their efforts. What I really object to is their illusion that, if they were successful, if the identity of the Friend, the Dark Lady, the Rival Poet, etc., could be established beyond doubt, this would in any way illuminate our understanding of the sonnets themselves.

Their illusion seems to me to betray either a complete misunderstanding of the nature of the relation between art and life or an attempt to rationalize and justify plain vulgar idle curiosity.

Idle curiosity is an ineradicable vice of the human mind. All of us like to discover the secrets of our neighbors, particularly the ugly ones. This has always been so, and, probably, always will be. What is relatively new, however —it is scarcely to be found before the latter half of the eighteenth century—is a blurring of the borderline between the desire for truth and idle curiosity, until, today, it has been so thoroughly erased that we can indulge in the latter without the slightest pangs of conscience. A great deal of what today passes for scholarly research is an activity no different from that of reading somebody's private correspondence when he is out of the room, and it doesn't really make it morally any better if he is out of the room because he is in his grave.

In the case of a man of action—a ruler, a statesman, a general—the man is identical with his biography. In the case of any kind of artist, however, who is a maker not a doer, his biography, the story of his life, and the history of his works are distinct. In the case of a man of action, we can distinguish in a rough and ready way between his private personal life and his public life, but both are lives of action and, therefore, capable of affecting each other. The political interests of a king's mistress, for example, may influence his decisions on national policy. Consequently, the historian, in his search for truth, is justified in investigating the private life of a man of action to the degree that such discoveries throw light upon the history of his times which he had a share in shaping, even if the victim would prefer such secrets not to be known.

The case of any artist is quite different. Art history, the comparison of one work with another, one artistic epoch with another, the study of influences and changes of style is a legitimate study. The late J. B. Leishman's book, *Themes and Variations in Shakespeare's Sonnets,* is an admirable example of such an enquiry. Even the biography of an artist, if his life as a man was sufficiently interesting, is permissible, provided that the biographer and his readers realize that such an account throws no light whatsoever upon the artist's work. The relation between his life and his works is at one and the same time too self-evident to require comment—every work of art is, in one sense, a self-disclosure—and too complicated ever to unravel. Thus, it is self-evident that Catullus's love for Lesbia was the experience which inspired his love poems, and that, if either of them had had a different character, the poems would have been different, but no amount of research into their lives can tell us why Catullus wrote the actual poems he did, instead of an infinite number of similar poems he might have written instead, why, indeed he wrote any, or why those he did are good. Even if one could question a poet himself about the relation between some poem of his and the events which provoked him to write it, he could not give a satisfactory answer, because even the most "occasional" poem, in the Goethean sense, involves not only the occasion but the whole life experience of the poet, and he himself cannot identify all the contributing elements.

Further, it should be borne in mind that most genuine artists would prefer that no biography be written. A genuine artist believes he has been put on earth to fulfill a certain function determined by the talent with which he has been entrusted. His personal life is, naturally, of concern to himself and, he hopes, to his personal friends, but he does not think it is or ought to be of any concern to the public. The one thing a writer, for example, hopes for, is attentive readers of his writings. He hopes they will study the text closely enough to spot misprints. Shakespeare would be grateful to many scholars, beginning with Malone, who have suggested sensible emendations to the Q text. And he hopes that they will read with patience and intelligence so as to extract as much meaning from the text as possible. If the shade of Shakespeare has read Professor William Empson's explication of "They that have power to hurt and will do none" (Sonnet 94), he may have wondered to himself, "Now, did I *really* say all that?", but he will certainly be grateful to Mr. Empson for his loving care.

Not only would most genuine writers prefer to have no biography written; they would also prefer, were it practically feasible, that their writings were published anonymously.

Shakespeare is in the singularly fortunate position of being, to all intents and purposes, anonymous. Hence the existence of persons who spend their lives trying to prove that his plays were written by someone else. (How odd it is that Freud should have been a firm believer in the Earl of Oxford theory.)

So far as the sonnets are concerned, the certain facts are just two in number. Two of the sonnets, "When my love swears that she is made of truth" (138), and "Two loves I have, of comfort and despair" (144), appeared in *The Passionate Pilgrim,* a poetic miscellany printed in 1599, and the whole collection was published by G. Eld for T. T. in 1609 with a dedication "To.The.Onlie.Begetter.Of. These.Insuing.Sonnets. Mr. W.H." Meres's reference in 1598 to "sugred Sonnets" by Shakespeare is inconclusive: the word *sonnet* was often used as a general term for a lyric, and even if Meres was using it in the stricter sense, we do not know if the sonnets he was referring to are the ones we have.

Aside from the text itself, this is all we know for certain and all we are ever likely to know. On philological grounds, I am inclined to agree with those scholars who take the word *begetter* to mean procurer, so that Mr. W.H. is not the friend who inspired most of the sonnets, but the person who secured the manuscript for the publisher.

So far as the date of their composition is concerned, all we know for certain is that the relation between Shakespeare and the Friend lasted at least three years:

> Three April perfumes in three hot Junes burned,
> Since first I saw you fresh, which yet are green. (104)

The fact that the style of the sonnets is nearer to that of the earlier plays than the later is not conclusive proof that their composition was contemporary with the former, because a poet's style is always greatly influenced by the particular verse form he is employing. As Professor C. S. Lewis has said: "If Shakespeare had taken an hour off from the composition of *Lear* to write a sonnet, the sonnet might not have been in the style of *Lear*." On the whole, I think an early date is a more plausible conjecture than a late one, because the experiences the sonnets describe seem to me to be more likely to befall a younger man than an older.

Let us, however, forget all about Shakespeare the man, leave the speculations about the persons involved, the names, already or in the future to be put forward, South-ampton, Pembroke, Hughes, etc., to the foolish and the idle, and consider the sonnets themselves.

The first thing which is obvious after reading through the one hundred and fifty-four sonnets as we have them, is that they are not in any kind of planned sequence. The only semblance of order is a division into two unequal heaps—Sonnets 1 to 126 are addressed to a young man, assuming, which is probable but not certain, that there is only one young man addressed, and Sonnets 127–154 are addressed to a dark-haired woman. In both heaps, a triangle situation is referred to in which Shakespeare's friend and his mistress betray him by having an affair together, which proves that the order is not chronological. Sonnets 40 and 42, "Take all my loves, my love, yea take them all," "That thou hast her, it is not all my grief," must be more or less contemporary with 144 and 152, "Two loves I have, of comfort and despair," "In loving thee thou know'st I am forsworn."

Nor in the two sets considered separately is it possible to believe that the order is chronological. Sometimes batches of sonnets occur which clearly belong together—for example, the opening series 1–17, in which the friend is urged to marry, though, even here, 15 seems not to belong, for marriage is not mentioned in it. At other times, sonnets which are similar in theme are widely separated. To take a very trivial example. In 77 Shakespeare speaks of giving his friend a commonplace book.

> Look what thy memory cannot contain,
> Commit to these waste blanks.

And in 122, he speaks of a similar gift from his friend to him,

> Thy gift, thy tables, are within my brain.

Surely, it is probable that they exchanged gifts and that these sonnets belong together.

The serious objection, however, to the order of Sonnets 1–126 as the Q text prints them is psychological. Sonnets expressing feelings of unalloyed happiness and devotion are mixed with others expressing grief and estrangement. Some speak of injuries done to Shakespeare by his friend, others of some scandal in which the friend was involved, others again of some infidelity on Shakespeare's part in a succession which makes no kind of emotional sense.

Any passionate relationship can go through and survive painful crises, and become all the stronger for it. As Shakespeare writes in Sonnet 119:

> O, benefit of ill: now I find true
> That better is by evil still made better;
> And ruined love, when it is built anew,
> Grows fairer than at first, more strong, far greater.

But forgiveness and reconciliation do not obliterate memory of the past. It is not possible to return to the innocent happiness expressed before any cloud appeared on the sky. It is not, it seems to me, possible to believe that, *after* going through the experiences described in Sonnets 40–42, Shakespeare would write either Sonnet 53,

> In all external grace, you have some part,
> But you like none, none you, for constant heart

or 105,

> Let not my love be called idolatry,
> Nor my beloved as an idol show,
> Since all alike my songs and praises be
> To one, of one, still such, and ever so.
> Kind is my love today, tomorrow kind,
> Still constant in a wondrous excellence.

If the order is not chronological, it cannot, either, be a sequence planned by Shakespeare for publication. Any writer with an audience in mind knows that a sequence of poems must climax with one of the best. Yet the sequence as we have it concludes with two of the worst of the sonnets, trivial conceits about, apparently, going to Bath to take the waters. Nor, when preparing for publication, will an author leave unrevised what is obviously a first draft, like Sonnet 99 with its fifteen lines.

A number of scholars have tried to rearrange the sonnets into some more logical order, but such efforts can never be more than conjecture, and it is best to accept the jumble we have been given.

If the first impression made by the sonnets is of their haphazard order, the second is of their extremely uneven poetic value.

After the 1609 edition, the sonnets were pretty well forgotten for over a century and a half. In 1640 Benson produced an extraordinary hodgepodge in which one hundred and forty-six of them were arranged into seventy-two poems with invented titles, and some of the *he*'s and *him*'s changed to *she*'s and *her*'s. It was not until 1780 that a significant critical text was made by Malone. This happened to be a period when critics condemned the sonnet as a form. Thus Steevens could write in 1766:

> Quaintness, obscurity, and tautology are to be regarded as the constituent parts of this exotic species of composition. . . . I am one of those who should have wished it to have expired in the country where it was born. . . . [A sonnet] is composed in the highest strain of affectation, pedantry, circumlocution, and nonsense.

And of Shakespeare's essays in this form:

> The strongest act of Parliament that could be framed would fail to compel readers unto their service.

Even when this prejudice against the sonnet as such had begun to weaken, and even after Bardolatry had begun, adverse criticism of the sonnets continued.

Thus Wordsworth, who was as responsible as anyone for rehabilitating the sonnet as a form (though he employed the Petrarchan, not the Shakespearean, kind), remarked:

> These sonnets beginning at CXXVII to his mistress are worse than a puzzle-peg. They are abominably harsh, obscure, and worthless. The others are for the most part much better, have many fine lines and passages. They are

also in many places warm with passion. Their chief faults—and heavy ones they are—are sameness, tediousness, quaintness, and elaborate obscurity.

Hazlitt:

If Shakespeare had written nothing but his sonnets . . . he would . . . have been assigned to the class of cold, artificial writers, who had no genuine sense of nature or passion.

Keats:

They seem to be full of fine things said unintentionally— in the intensity of working out conceits.

Landor:

Not a single one is very admirable. . . . They are hot and pothery: there is much condensation, little delicacy; like raspberry jam without cream, without crust, without bread; to break its viscidity.

In this century we have reacquired a taste for the conceit, as we have for baroque architecture, and no longer think that artifice is incompatible with passion. Even so, no serious critic of poetry can possibly think that all the sonnets are equally good.

On going through the hundred and fifty-four of them, I find forty-nine which seem to me excellent throughout, a good number of the rest have one or two memorable lines, but there are also several which I can only read out of a sense of duty. For the inferior ones we have no right to condemn Shakespeare unless we are prepared to believe, a belief for which there is no evidence, that he prepared or intended them all to be published.

Considered in the abstract, as if they were Platonic Ideas, the Petrarchan sonnet seems to be a more esthetically satisfying form than the Shakespearean. Having only two different rhymes in the octave and two in the sestet, each is bound by rhyme into a closed unity, and the asymmetrical relation of 8 to 6 is pleasing. The Shakespearean form, on the other hand, with its seven different rhymes, almost inevitably becomes a lyric of three symmetrical quatrains, finished off with an epigrammatic couplet. As a rule Shakespeare shapes his rhetorical argument in conformity with this, that is to say, there is usually a major pause after the fourth, the eighth, and the twelfth line. Only in one case, Sonnet 86, "Was it the proud full sail of his great verse," does the main pause occur in the middle of the second quatrain, so that the sonnet divides into 6.6.2.

It is the concluding couplet in particular which, in the Shakespearean form, can be a snare. The poet is tempted to use it, either to make a summary of the preceding twelve lines which is unnecessary, or to draw a moral which is too glib and trite. In the case of Shakespeare himself, though there are some wonderful couplets, for example the conclusion of 61,

> For thee watch I, whilst thou dost wake elsewhere,
> From me far off, with others all too near,

or 87,

> Thus have I had thee as a dream doth flatter,
> In sleep a king, but waking no such matter,

all too often, even in some of the best, the couplet lines are the weakest and dullest in the sonnet, and, coming where they do at the end, the reader has the sense of a disappointing anticlimax.

Despite all this, it seems to me wise of Shakespeare to have chosen the form he did rather than the Petrarchan. Compared with Italian, English is so poor in rhymes that it is almost impossible to write a Petrarchan sonnet in it that sounds effortless throughout. In even the best examples from Milton, Wordsworth, Rossetti, for example, one is almost sure to find at least one line the concluding word of which does not seem inevitable, the only word which could accurately express the poet's meaning; one feels it is only there because the rhyme demanded it.

In addition, there are certain things which can be done in the Shakespearean form which the Petrarchan, with its sharp division between octave and sestet, cannot do. In Sonnet 66, "Tired with all these, for restful death I cry," and 129, "Th' expense of spirit in a waste of shame," Shakespeare is able to give twelve single-line *exempla* of the wretchedness of this world and the horrors of lust, with an accumulative effect of great power.

In their style, two characteristics of the sonnets stand out. Firstly, their *cantabile*. They are the work of someone whose ear is unerring. In his later blank verse, Shakespeare became a master of highly complicated effects of sound and rhythm, and the counterpointing of these with the sense, but in the sonnets he is intent upon making his verse as melodious, in the simplest and most obvious sense of the word, as possible, and there is scarcely a line, even in the dull ones, which sounds harsh or awkward. Occasionally, there are lines which foreshadow the freedom of his later verse. For example:

> Not mine own fears nor the prophetic soul
> Of the wide world dreaming on things to come. (107)

But, as a rule, he keeps the rhythm pretty close to the metrical base. Inversion, except in the first foot, is rare, and so is trisyllabic substitution. The commonest musical devices are alliteration—

> Then were not summer's distillation left,
> A liquid prisoner pent in walls of glass   (5)

> Let me not to the marriage of true minds
> Admit impediments . . .   (116)

and the careful patterning of long and short vowels—

> How many a holy and obsequious tear   (31)

> Nor think the bitterness of absence sour   (57)

> So far from home into my deeds to pry.   (61)

The second characteristic they display is a mastery of

every possible rhetorical device. The reiteration, for example, of words with either an identical or a different meaning—

> love is not love
> Which alters when it alteration finds,
> Or bends with the remover to remove. (116)

Or the avoidance of monotony by an artful arithmetical variation of theme or illustration.

Here, I cannot do better than to quote (interpolating lines where appropriate) Professor C. S. Lewis on Sonnet 18. "As often," he says, "the theme begins at line 9,

> But thy eternal summer shall not fade,

occupying four lines, and the application is in the couplet:

> So long as men can breathe or eyes can see,
> So long lives this, and this gives life to thee.

Line 1

> Shall I compare thee to a summer's day

proposes a simile. Line 2

> Thou art more lively and more temperate

corrects it. Then we have two one-line *exempla* justifying the correction

> Rough winds do shake the darling buds of May,
> And summer's lease hath all too short a date:

then a two-line *exemplum* about the sun

> Sometime too hot the eye of heaven shines,
> And often is his gold complexion dimmed:

then two more lines

> And every fair from fair sometime declines,
> By chance, or nature's changing course, untrimmed

which do not, as we had expected, add a fourth *exemplum*
but generalize. Equality of length in the two last variations
is thus played off against difference of function."[1]

The visual imagery is usually drawn from the most ob-
viously beautiful natural objects, but, in a number, a single
metaphorical conceit is methodically worked out, as in 87,

> Farewell, thou art too dear for my possessing,

where the character of an emotional relationship is worked
out in terms of a legal contract.

In the inferior sonnets, such artifices may strike the
reader as artificial, but he must reflect that, without the
artifice, they might be much worse than they are. The
worst one can say, I think, is that rhetorical skill enables
a poet to write a poem for which genuine inspiration is
lacking which, had he lacked such skill, he would not have
written at all.

On the other hand those sonnets which express passionate
emotions, whether of adoration or anger or grief or disgust,
owe a very great deal of their effect precisely to Shake-
peare's artifice, for without the restraint and distancing
which the rhetorical devices provide, the intensity and im-
mediacy of the emotion might have produced, not a poem,
but an embarrassing "human document." Wordsworth de-
fined poetry as emotion recollected in tranquillity. It seems
highly unlikely that Shakespeare wrote many of these son-
nets out of recollected emotion. In his case, it is the artifice
that makes up for the lack of tranquillity.

If the vagueness of the historical circumstances under
which the sonnets were written has encouraged the goats
of idle curiosity, their matter has given the goats of ideology
a wonderful opportunity to display their love of simplifica-
tion at the expense of truth. Confronted with the extremely
odd story they tell, with the fact that, in so many of them,
Shakespeare addresses a young man in terms of passionate
devotion, the sound and sensible citizen, alarmed at the

[1] *English Literature in the Sixteenth Century.* Oxford: Clarendon Press,
1954, p. 507.

thought that our Top-Bard could have had any experience with which he is unfamiliar, has either been shocked and wished that Shakespeare had never written them, or, in defiance of common sense, tried to persuade himself that Shakespeare was merely expressing in somewhat hyperbolic terms, such as an Elizabethan poet might be expected to use, what any normal man feels for a friend of his own sex. The homosexual reader, on the other hand, determined to secure our Top-Bard as a patron saint of the Homintern, has been uncritically enthusiastic about the first one hundred and twenty-six of the sonnets, and preferred to ignore those to the Dark Lady in which the relationship is unequivocally sexual, and the fact that Shakespeare was a married man and a father.

Dag Hammerskjöld, in a diary found after his death and just recently published in Sweden, makes an observation to which both the above types would do well to listen.

> How easy Psychology has made it for us to dismiss the perplexing mystery with a label which assigns it a place in the list of common aberrations.

That we are confronted in the sonnets by a mystery rather than by an aberration is evidenced for me by the fact that men and women whose sexual tastes are perfectly normal, but who enjoy and understand poetry, have always been able to read them as expressions of what they understand by the word *love,* without finding the masculine pronoun an obstacle.

I think that the *primary* experience—complicated as it became later—out of which the sonnets to the friend spring was a mystical one.

All experiences which may be called mystical have certain characteristics in common.

(1) The experience is "given." That is to say, it cannot be induced or prolonged by an effort of will, though the openness of any individual to receive it is partly determined by his age, his psychophysical make-up, and his cultural milieu.

(2) Whatever the contents of the experience, the sub-

ject is absolutely convinced that it is a revelation of reality. When it is over, he does not say, as one says when one awakes from a dream: "Now I am awake and conscious again of the real world." He says, rather: "For a while the veil was lifted and a reality revealed which in my 'normal' state is hidden from me."

(3) With whatever the vision is concerned, things, human beings, or God, they are experienced as numinous, clothed in glory, charged with an intense being-thereness.

(4) Confronted by the vision, the attention of the subject, in awe, joy, dread, is absolutely absorbed in contemplation and, while the vision lasts, his self, its desires and needs, are completely forgotten.

Natural mystical experiences, visions that is to say, concerned with created beings, not with a creator God, and without overt religious content, are of two kinds, which one might call the Vision of Dame Kind and the Vision of Eros.

The classic descriptions of the first are to be found, of course, in certain of Wordsworth's poems, like *The Prelude,* the Immortality Ode, "Tintern Abbey," and "The Ruined Cottage." It is concerned with a multiplicity of creatures, inanimate and animate, but not with persons, though it may include human artifacts. If human beings do appear in it, they are always, I believe, total strangers to the subject, so that, so far as he is concerned, they are not persons. It would seem that, in our culture, this vision is not uncommon in childhood, but rare in adults.

The Vision of Eros, on the other hand, is concerned with a single person, who is revealed to the subject as being of infinite sacred importance. The classic descriptions of it are to be found in Plato's *Symposium,* Dante's *La Vita Nuova,* and some of these sonnets by Shakespeare.

It can, it seems, be experienced before puberty. If it occurs later, though the subject is aware of its erotic nature, his own desire is always completely subordinate to the sacredness of the beloved person who is felt to be infinitely superior to the lover. Before anything else, the lover desires the happiness of the beloved.

The Vision of Eros is probably a much rarer experience than most people in our culture suppose, but, when it is genuine, I do not think it makes any sense to apply to it terms like heterosexual or homosexual. Such terms can only be legitimately applied to the profane erotic experiences with which we are all familiar, to lust, for example, an interest in another solely as a sexual object, and that combination of sexual desire and *philia,* affection based upon mutual interests, values, and shared experiences which is the securest basis for a happy marriage.

That, in the Vision of Eros, the erotic is the medium, not the cause, is proved, I think, by the fact, on which all who have written about it with authority agree, that it cannot long survive an actual sexual relationship. Indeed, it is very doubtful if the Vision can ever be mutual: the story of Tristan and Isolde is a myth, not an instance of what can historically occur. To be receptive to it, it would seem that the subject must be exceptionally imaginative. Class feelings also seem to play a role; no one, apparently, can have such a vision about an individual who belongs to a social group which he has been brought up to regard as inferior to his own, so that its members are not, for him, fully persons.

The medium of the Vision is, however, undoubtedly erotic. Nobody who was unconscious of an erotic interest on his part would use the frank, if not brutal, sexual image which Shakespeare employs in speaking of his friend's exclusive interest in women.

> But since she pricked thee out for women's pleasure,
> Mine be thy love, and thy love's use their treasure. (20)

The beloved is always beautiful in the impersonal sense of the word as well as the personal. It is unfortunate that we have to use the same words, beauty and beautiful, to mean two quite different things. If I say: "Elizabeth has a beautiful figure" or "a beautiful profile," I am referring to an objective, publicly recognizable property, and, so long as the objects are members of the same class, I can compare one with another and arrange them along a scale of beauty. That is why it is possible to hold dog shows, beauty competitions, etc., or for a sculptor to state in mathematical terms the proportions of the ideal male or female figure. This kind of beauty is a gift of Nature's, depending upon a lucky combination of genes and the luck of good health, and a gift which Nature can, and, in due time, always does, take away. The reaction of the spectactor to it is either impersonal admiration or impersonal sexual desire. Moral approval is not involved. It is perfectly possible for me to say: "Elizabeth has a beautiful figure, but she is a monster."

If, on the other hand, I say: "Elizabeth has a beautiful face or a beautiful expression," though I am still referring to something physical—I could not make the statement if I were blind—I am speaking of something which is personal, a unique face which cannot be compared with that of anyone else, and for which I hold Elizabeth personally responsible. Nature has had nothing to do with it. This kind of beauty is always associated with the notion of moral goodness. It is impossible to imagine circumstances in which I could say: "Elizabeth has a beautiful expression but she is a monster." And it is this kind of beauty which arouses in the beholder feelings, not of impersonal admiration or lust, but of personal love.

The Petrarchan distinction, employed by Shakespeare in a number of his sonnets, between the love of the eye and the love of the heart, is an attempt, I think, to express the difference between these two kinds of beauty and our response to them.

In the Vision of Eros, both are always present. The beloved is always beautiful in both the public and the personal sense. But, to the lover, the second is the more important. Dante certainly thought that Beatrice was a girl whose beauty everybody would admire, but it wouldn't have entered his head to compare her for beauty with other Florentine girls of the same age.

Both Plato and Dante attempt to give a religious explanation of the Vision. Both, that is to say, regard the love inspired by a created human being as intended to lead the lover towards the love of the uncreated source of all beauty. The difference between them is that Plato is without any notion of what we mean by a person, whether human or Divine; he can only think in terms of the individual and the universal, and beauty, for him, is always beauty in the impersonal sense. Consequently, on the Platonic ladder, the love of an individual must be forgotten in the love of the universal; what we should call infidelity becomes a moral duty. How different is Dante's interpretation. Neither he nor Beatrice tells us exactly what he had done which had led him to the brink of perdition, but both speak of it as a lack of fidelity on Dante's part to his love for Beatrice. In Paradise, she is with him up until the final moment when he turns from her towards "The Eternal Fountain" and, even then, he knows that her eyes are turned in the same direction. Instead of the many rungs of the Platonic ladder, there is only one step for the lover to take, from the person of the beloved creature to the Person of their common Creator.

It is consistent with Shakespeare's cast of mind as we meet it in the plays, where it is impossible to be certain what his personal beliefs were on any subject, that the sonnets should contain no theory of love: Shakespeare contents himself with simply describing the experience.

Though the primary experience from which they started was, I believe, the Vision of Eros, that is, of course, not all they are about. For the vision to remain undimmed, it is probably necessary that the lover have very little contact with the beloved, however nice a person she (or he) may be. Dante, after all, only saw Beatrice once or twice, and she probably knew little about him. The story of the sonnets seems to me to be the story of an agonized struggle by Shakespeare to preserve the glory of the vision he had been granted in a relationship, lasting at least three years, with a person who seemed intent by his actions upon covering the vision with dirt.

As outsiders, the impression we get of his friend is one of a young man who was not really very nice, very conscious of his good looks, able to switch on the charm at any moment, but essentially frivolous, cold-hearted, and self-centered, aware, probably, that he had some power over Shakespeare—if he thought about it at all, no doubt he gave it a cynical explanation—but with no conception of the intensity of the feelings he had, unwittingly, aroused. Somebody, in fact, rather like Bassanio in *The Merchant of Venice*.

The sonnets addressed to the Dark Lady are concerned with that most humiliating of all erotic experiences, sexual infatuation—*Vénus toute entière à sa proie attachée*.

Simple lust is impersonal, that is to say the pursuer regards himself as a person but the object of his pursuit as a thing, to whose personal qualities, if she has any, he is indifferent, and, if he succeeds, he expects to be able to make a safe getaway as soon as he becomes bored. Sometimes, however, he gets trapped. Instead of becoming bored, he becomes sexually obsessed, and the girl, instead of conveniently remaining an object, becomes a real person to him, but a person whom he not only does not love, but actively dislikes.

No other poet, not even Catullus, has described the anguish, self-contempt, and rage produced by this unfortunate condition so well as Shakespeare in some of these sonnets, 141, for example, "In faith I do not love thee with my eyes," or 151, "Love is too young to know what conscience is."

Aside from the opening sixteen sonnets urging his friend to marry—which may well, as some scholars have suggested, have been written at the suggestion of some member of the young man's family—aside from these, and half a dozen elegant trifles, what is astonishing about the sonnets, especially when one remembers the age in which they were written, is the impression they make of naked autobiographical confession. The Elizabethans were not given to writing their autobiographies or to "unlocking their hearts." Donne's love poems were no doubt inspired by a personal passion, but this is hidden behind the public performance. It is not until Rousseau and the age of *Sturm und Drang* that confession becomes a literary genre. After the sonnets, I cannot think of anything in English poetry so seemingly autobiographical until Meredith's *Modern Love*,

and even then, the personal events seem to be very care-
fully "posed."

It is impossible to believe either that Shakespeare wished
them to be published or that he can have shown most of
them to the young man and woman, whoever they were,
to whom they are addressed. Suppose you had written
Sonnet 57,

> Being your slave, what should I do but tend
> Upon the hours and times of your desire?

Can you imagine showing it to the person you were think-
ing of? Vice versa, what on earth would you feel, supposing
someone you knew handed you the sonnet and said: "This
is about you"?

Though Shakespeare may have shown the sonnets to
one or two intimate literary friends—it would appear that
he must have—he wrote them, I am quite certain, as one
writes a diary, for himself alone, with no thought of a public.

When the sonnets are really obscure, they are obscure
in the way that a diary can be, in which the writer does
not bother to explain references which are obvious to him,
but an outsider cannot know. For example, in the opening
lines of Sonnet 125

> Were't aught to me I bore the canopy,
> With my extern the outward honoring.

It is impossible for the reader to know whether Shakespeare
is simply being figurative or whether he is referring to some
ceremony in which he actually took part, or, if he is, what
that ceremony can have been. Again, the concluding coup-
let of 124 remains impenetrable.

> To this I witness call the fools of Time,
> Which die for goodness, who have lived for crime.

Some critics have suggested that this is a cryptic reference
to the Jesuits who were executed on charges of high treason.
This may be so, but there is nothing in the text to prove it,
and even if it is so, I fail to understand their relevance as
witnesses to Shakespeare's love which no disaster or self-
interest can affect.

How the sonnets came to be published—whether Shakespeare gave copies to some friend who then betrayed him, or whether some enemy stole them—we shall probably never know. Of one thing I am certain: Shakespeare must have been horrified when they were published.

The Elizabethan age was certainly as worldly-wise and no more tolerant, perhaps less, than our own. After all, sodomy was still a capital offense. The poets of the period, like Marlowe and Barnfield, whom we know to have been homosexual, were very careful not to express their feelings in the first person, but in terms of classical mythology. Renaissance Italy had the reputation for being tolerant on this subject, yet, when Michelangelo's nephew published his sonnets to Tomasso de Cavalieri, which are much more restrained than Shakespeare's, for the sake of his uncle's reputation he altered the sex, just as Benson was to do with Shakespeare in 1640.

Shakespeare must have known that his sonnets would be read by many readers in 1609 as they are read by many today—with raised eyebrows. Though I believe such a reaction to be due to a misunderstanding, one cannot say that it is not understandable.

In our culture, we have good reason to be skeptical when anyone claims to have experienced the Vision of Eros, and even to doubt if it ever occurs, because half our literature, popular and highbrow, ever since the Provençal poets made the disastrous mistake of trying to turn a mystical experience into a social cult, is based on the assumption that what is, probably, a rare experience, is one which almost everybody has or ought to have; if they don't, then there must be something wrong with them. We know only too well how often, when a person speaks of having "fallen in love" with X, what he or she really feels could be described in much cruder terms. As La Rochefoucauld observed:

> True love is like seeing ghosts: we all talk about it, but few of us have ever seen one.

It does not follow, however, that true love or ghosts cannot exist. Perhaps poets are more likely to experience it than others, or become poets because they have. Perhaps Hannah Arendt is right: "Poets are the only people to whom love is not only a crucial but an indispensable experience, which entitles them to mistake it for a universal one." In Shakespeare's case, what happened to his relations with his friend and his mistress, whether they were abruptly broken off in a quarrel, or slowly faded into indifference, is anybody's guess. Did Shakespeare later feel that the anguish at the end was not too great a price to pay for the glory of the initial vision? I hope so and believe so. Anyway, poets are tough and can profit from the most dreadful experiences.

There is a scene in *The Two Noble Kinsmen* which most scholars believe to have been written by Shakespeare and which, if he did, may very well be the last thing he wrote. In it there is a speech by Palamon in which he prays to Venus for her aid. The speech is remarkable, firstly, in its choice of examples of the power of the Goddess—nearly all are humiliating or horrid—and, secondly, for the intensity of the disgust expressed at masculine sexual vanity.

> Hail, Sovereign Queen of secrets, who has power
> To call the fiercest tyrant from his rage,
> And weep unto a girl; that hast the might
> Even with an eye-glance, to choke Mars's drum
> And turn th' alarm to whispers; that canst make
> A cripple flourish with his crutch, and cure him
> Before Apollo; that mayst force the King
> To be his subjects' vassal, and induce
> Stale gravity to dance; the polled bachelor—
> Whose youth, like wanton boys through bonfires,
> Have skipped thy flame—at seventy thou canst catch
> And make him, to the scorn of his hoarse throat,
> Abuse young lays of love: what godlike power
> Hast thou not power upon? . . .
>   . . . Take to thy grace
> Me, thy vowed soldier, who do bear thy yoke
> As 'twere a wreath of roses, yet is heavier
> Than lead itself, stings more than nettles.
> I have never been foul-mouthed against thy law,
> Nev'r revealed secret, for I knew none; would not

Had I kenned all that were; I never practised
Upon man's wife, nor would the libels read
Of liberal wits; I never at great feasts
Sought to betray a beauty, but have blushed
At simp'ring Sirs that did; I have been harsh
To large confessors, and have hotly asked them
If they had mothers: I had one, a woman,
And women 'twere they wronged. I knew a man
Of eighty winters, this I told them, who
A lass of fourteen brided. 'Twas thy power
To put life into dust; the aged cramp
Had screwed his square foot round,
The gout had knitted his fingers into knots,
Torturing convulsions from his globy eyes,
Had almost drawn their spheres, that what was life
In him seemed torture: this anatomy
Had by his young fair pheare a boy, and I
Believed it was his, for she swore it was,
And who would not believe her? Brief, I am
To those that prate, and have done, no companion;
To those that boast, and have not, a defier;
To those that would, and cannot, a rejoicer.
Yea, him I do not love, that tells close offices
The foulest way, nor names concealments in
The boldest language. Such a one I am,
And vow that lover never yet made sigh
Truer than I. O, then, most soft, sweet Goddess,
Give me the victory of this question, which
Is true love's merit, and bless me with a sign
Of thy great pleasure.

*Here music is heard, doves are seen to flutter; they fall again
upon their faces, then on their knees.*

Oh thou, that from eleven to ninety reign'st
In mortal bosoms, whose chase is this world,
And we in herds thy game; I give thee thanks
For this fair token, which, being laid unto
Mine innocent true heart, arms in assurance
My body to this business. Let us rise
And bow before the Goddess: Time comes on.

         Exeunt. Still music of records.

            W. H. AUDEN

TO THE ONLY BEGETTER OF

THESE ENSUING SONNETS

MR. W. H. ALL HAPPINESS

AND THAT ETERNITY

PROMISED

BY

OUR EVER-LIVING POET

WISHETH

THE WELL-WISHING

ADVENTURER IN

SETTING

FORTH

T. T.

The initials concluding the dedication are those of Thomas Thorpe, the publisher of the volume. The identity of Mr. W. H. is uncertain. Most persons who write on the subject have felt it too prosaic to hold that Mr. W. H. was simply a person who brought the poems into the publisher's hands; rather, they have sought to identify him with the friend to whom many of the poems are addressed. The favorite candidates are William Herbert, Earl of Pembroke (and one of the dedicatees of the First Folio), and Henry Wriothesley, Earl of Southampton (to whom Shakespeare dedicated *Venus and Adonis* and *Lucrece*). But it is unlikely that an earl would be addressed as "Mr." Yet another candidate is Sir William Hervey, third husband of Southampton's mother; his advocates say that Hervey was the "begetter" in the sense that he may have encouraged Shakespeare to write the sonnets urging the young man (allegedly Southampton) to wed.

1

From fairest creatures we desire increase,
That thereby beauty's rose might never die,
But as the riper should by time decease,
His tender heir might bear his memory;   4
But thou contracted to thine own bright eyes,
Feed'st thy light's flame with self-substantial fuel,
Making a famine where abundance lies,
Thyself thy foe, to thy sweet self too cruel.   8
Thou that art now the world's fresh ornament,
And only herald to the gaudy spring,
Within thine own bud buriest thy content,
And, tender churl, mak'st waste in niggarding.   12
   Pity the world, or else this glutton be,
    To eat the world's due, by the grave and thee.

5 *contracted* betrothed   6 *self-substantial fuel* fuel of your own substance   10 *only* chief   11 *thy content* what you contain, i.e., potential fatherhood   12 *niggarding* hoarding   14 *world's due* i.e., propagation of the species   14 *by the grave and thee* i.e., by dying without children

2

When forty winters shall besiege thy brow,
And dig deep trenches in thy beauty's field,
Thy youth's proud livery, so gazed on now,
4   Will be a tottered weed of small worth held:
Then being asked where all thy beauty lies,
Where all the treasure of thy lusty days,
To say within thine own deep-sunken eyes,
8   Were an all-eating shame and thriftless praise.
How much more praise deserved thy beauty's use,
If thou couldst answer, "This fair child of mine
Shall sum my count, and make my old excuse,"
12   Proving his beauty by succession thine.
    This were to be new made when thou art old,
    And see thy blood warm when thou feel'st it cold.

2 *trenches* i.e., wrinkles   3 *livery* outward appearance   4 *tottered weed* tattered garment   6 *lusty* vigorous   8 *thriftless* unprofitable   9 *use* investment   11 *sum my count* even out my account   11 *my old excuse* excuse when I am old

3

Look in thy glass and tell the face thou viewest
Now is the time that face should form another,
Whose fresh repair if now thou not renewest,
Thou dost beguile the world, unbless some mother.   4
For where is she so fair whose uneared womb
Disdains the tillage of thy husbandry?
Or who is he so fond will be the tomb
Of his self-love to stop posterity?   8
Thou art thy mother's glass, and she in thee
Calls back the lovely April of her prime;
So thou through windows of thine age shalt see,
Despite of wrinkles, this thy golden time.   12
    But if thou live rememb'red not to be,
    Die single and thine image dies with thee.

3 *fresh repair* youthful state   4 *unbless some mother* leave some woman unblessed with motherhood   5 *uneared* untilled   7 *fond* foolish   8 *Of* because of   13 *rememb'red not to be* only to be forgotten

4

Unthrifty loveliness, why dost thou spend
Upon thyself thy beauty's legacy?
Nature's bequest gives nothing but doth lend,
4   And being frank she lends to those are free.
Then, beauteous niggard, why dost thou abuse
The bounteous largess given thee to give?
Profitless usurer, why dost thou use
8   So great a sum of sums yet canst not live?
For having traffic with thyself alone,
Thou of thyself thy sweet self dost deceive.
Then how when Nature calls thee to be gone,
12 What acceptable audit canst thou leave?
        Thy unused beauty must be tombed with thee,
        Which, usèd, lives th' executor to be.

2 *beauty's legacy* inheritance of beauty   4 *frank . . . free* (both
words mean "generous")   5 *niggard* miser   7 *use* (1) invest
(2) use up   8 *live* (1) make a living (2) endure   9 *traffic* com-
merce   14 *lives* i.e., in a son

5

Those hours that with gentle work did frame
The lovely gaze where every eye doth dwell
Will play the tyrants to the very same
And that unfair which fairly doth excel;   *4*
For never-resting Time leads summer on
To hideous winter and confounds him there,
Sap checked with frost and lusty leaves quite gone,
Beauty o'ersnowed and bareness everywhere.   *8*
Then, were not summer's distillation left
A liquid prisoner pent in walls of glass,
Beauty's effect with beauty were bereft,
Nor it nor no remembrance what it was.   *12*
    But flowers distilled though they with winter meet,
    Leese but their show, their substance still lives
        sweet.

1 *hours* (disyllabic)   2 *gaze* object gazed on   4 *unfair* make
ugly   4 *fairly* in beauty   6 *confounds* destroys   9 *summer's dis-
tillation* perfumes made from flowers   11 *Beauty's effect* i.e., the
perfume   12 *Nor . . . nor* (there would be) neither . . . nor
14 *Leese but their show* lose only their outward form

6

Then let not winter's ragged hand deface
In thee thy summer ere thou be distilled.
Make sweet some vial; treasure thou some place
4   With beauty's treasure ere it be self-killed.
That use is not forbidden usury
Which happies those that pay the willing loan;
That's for thyself to breed another thee,
8   Or ten times happier be it ten for one.
Ten times thyself were happier than thou art,
If ten of thine ten times refigured thee:
Then what could death do if thou shouldst depart,
12   Leaving thee living in posterity?
    Be not self-willed, for thou art much too fair,
     To be death's conquest and make worms thine
       heir.

---

1 *ragged* rough   3 *treasure* enrich   5 *use* lending money at interest   6 *happies . . . loan* makes happy those who willingly pay the loan   9 *happier* luckier   10 *refigured* represented

7

Lo, in the orient when the gracious light
Lifts up his burning head, each under eye
Doth homage to his new-appearing sight,
Serving with looks his sacred majesty;   *4*
And having climbed the steep-up heavenly hill,
Resembling strong youth in his middle age,
Yet mortal looks adore his beauty still,
Attending on his golden pilgrimage;   *8*
But when from highmost pitch, with weary car,
Like feeble age he reeleth from the day,
The eyes, 'fore duteous, now converted are
From his low tract and look another way: *12*
   So thou, thyself outgoing in thy noon,
   Unlooked on diest unless thou get a son.

---

1 *orient* east   1 *light* sun   2 *under* i.e., earthly   7 *looks* onlookers   9 *highmost pitch* zenith   9 *car* chariot (of Phoebus)   11 *converted* turned away   12 *tract* track   14 *get* beget

8

Music to hear, why hear'st thou music sadly?
Sweets with sweets war not, joy delights in joy.
Why lov'st thou that which thou receiv'st not gladly,
4   Or else receiv'st with pleasure thine annoy?
If the true concord of well tunèd sounds,
By unions married, do offend thine ear,
They do but sweetly chide thee, who confounds
8   In singleness the parts that thou shouldst bear.
Mark how one string, sweet husband to another,
Strikes each in each by mutual ordering;
Resembling sire, and child, and happy mother,
12 Who all in one, one pleasing note do sing;
      Whose speechless song, being many, seeming one,
      Sings this to thee, "Thou single wilt prove none."

1 *Music to hear* you who are music to hear   1 *sadly* gravely
7–8 *confounds . . . bear* i.e., destroys by playing singly the mul-
tiple role (of husband and father) that you should play   9 *sweet
husband to another* i.e., tuned in unison (so that when struck, its
partner vibrates)   14 *none* nothing

9

Is it for fear to wet a widow's eye
That thou consum'st thyself in single life?
Ah, if thou issueless shalt hap to die,
The world will wail thee like a makeless wife;   *4*
The world will be thy widow and still weep,
That thou no form of thee hast left behind,
When every private widow well may keep,
By children's eyes, her husband's shape in mind.   *8*
Look what an unthrift in the world doth spend,
Shifts but his place, for still the world enjoys it;
But beauty's waste hath in the world an end,
And kept unused, the user so destroys it: *12*
   No love toward others in that bosom sits
   That on himself such murd'rous shame commits.

---

3 *issueless* childless   3 *hap* happen, chance   4 *makeless* mateless
5 *still* always   7 *private* individual   9 *Look what* whatever
9 *unthrift* prodigal   10 *his* its   14 *murd'rous shame* shameful
murder

10

For shame, deny that thou bear'st love to any
Who for thyself art so unprovident.
Grant if thou wilt, thou art beloved of many,
4   But that thou none lov'st is most evident;
For thou art so possessed with murd'rous hate,
That 'gainst thyself thou stick'st not to conspire,
Seeking that beauteous roof to ruinate,
8   Which to repair should be thy chief desire.
O, change thy thought, that I may change my mind.
Shall hate be fairer lodged than gentle love?
Be as thy presence is, gracious and kind,
12   Or to thyself at least kind-hearted prove.
     Make thee another self for love of me,
     That beauty still may live in thine or thee.

6 *thou stick'st* you scruple   7 *roof* i.e., body (which houses the
spirit)   11 *presence* appearance   14 *still* always

11

As fast as thou shalt wane, so fast thou grow'st
In one of thine, from that which thou departest;
And that fresh blood which youngly thou bestow'st
Thou mayst call thine, when thou from youth
    convertest.   *4*
Herein lives wisdom, beauty, and increase;
Without this, folly, age, and cold decay.
If all were minded so, the times should cease,
And threescore year would make the world away.   *8*
Let those whom Nature hath not made for store,
Harsh, featureless, and rude, barrenly perish.
Look whom she best endowed, she gave the more;
Which bounteous gift thou shouldst in bounty
    cherish.   *12*
  She carved thee for her seal, and meant thereby
  Thou shouldst print more, not let that copy die.

3 *youngly* in youth   4 *Thou . . . convertest* you . . . change
6 *Without this* beyond this course of action   7 *times* generations
of men   9 *for store* as stock to draw upon   10 *featureless, and*
rude ugly and unrefined   11 *Look whom* whomever   13 *seal*
stamp

12

When I do count the clock that tells the time,
And see the brave day sunk in hideous night;
When I behold the violet past prime,
4   And sable curls are silvered o'er with white;
When lofty trees I see barren of leaves,
Which erst from heat did canopy the herd,
And summer's green, all girded up in sheaves,
8   Borne on the bier with white and bristly beard;
Then of thy beauty do I question make,
That thou among the wastes of time must go,
Since sweets and beauties do themselves forsake,
12 And die as fast as they see others grow,
    And nothing 'gainst Time's scythe can make
        defense,
    Save breed, to brave him when he takes thee
        hence.

2 *brave* splendid   4 *sable* black   6 *erst* formerly   9 *question make* entertain doubt   14 *Save breed, to brave* except offspring, to defy

13

O, that you were yourself, but, love, you are
No longer yours than you yourself here live;
Against this coming end you should prepare,
And your sweet semblance to some other give.   *4*
So should that beauty which you hold in lease
Find no determination, then you were
Yourself again after your self's decease,
When your sweet issue your sweet form should bear.   *8*
Who lets so fair a house fall to decay,
Which husbandry in honor might uphold
Against the stormy gusts of winter's day
And barren rage of death's eternal cold?   *12*
    O, none but unthrifts! Dear my love, you know,
    You had a father; let your son say so.

---

3 *Against* in expectation of   5 *in lease* i.e., for a term   6 *deter-
mination* end   8 *issue* offspring   10 *husbandry* (1) thrift (2)
marriage   13 *unthrifts* prodigals

14

Not from the stars do I my judgment pluck,
And yet methinks I have astronomy;
But not to tell of good or evil luck,
4　Of plagues, of dearths, or seasons' quality;
Nor can I fortune to brief minutes tell,
Pointing to each his thunder, rain, and wind,
Or say with princes if it shall go well
8　By oft predict that I in heaven find.
But from thine eyes my knowledge I derive,
And, constant stars, in them I read such art
As truth and beauty shall together thrive
12　If from thyself to store thou wouldst convert:
　　Or else of thee this I prognosticate,
　　Thy end is truth's and beauty's doom and date.

1 *pluck* derive   2 *astronomy* astrology   5 *fortune to brief minutes tell* i.e., predict the exact time of each happening   6 *Pointing* appointing   6 *his* its   8 *oft predict that* frequent prediction of what   10 *art* knowledge   11 *As* as that   12 *store* fertility   12 *convert* turn   14 *doom and date* end, Judgment Day

15

When I consider everything that grows
Holds in perfection but a little moment,
That this huge stage presenteth naught but shows
Whereon the stars in secret influence comment;   *4*
When I perceive that men as plants increase,
Cheerèd and checked even by the selfsame sky,
Vaunt in their youthful sap, at height decrease,
And wear their brave state out of memory;   *8*
Then the conceit of this inconstant stay
Sets you most rich in youth before my sight,
Where wasteful Time debateth with Decay,
To change your day of youth to sullied night;   *12*
 And, all in war with Time for love of you,
 As he takes from you, I engraft you new.

4 *in secret influence comment* i.e., exert a silent influence
6 *Cheerèd and checked* encouraged and rebuked   7 *Vaunt*
boast   8 *wear their brave state out of memory* wear out their
handsome condition until it is forgotten   9 *conceit* idea   9 *stay*
duration   11 *debateth* contends   14 *engraft* i.e., with eternizing
poetry

16

But wherefore do not you a mightier way
Make war upon this bloody tyrant Time?
And fortify yourself in your decay
4 With means more blessèd than my barren rhyme?
Now stand you on the top of happy hours,
And many maiden gardens, yet unset,
With virtuous wish would bear your living flowers,
8 Much liker than your painted counterfeit.
So should the lines of life that life repair,
Which this time's pencil, or my pupil pen,
Neither in inward worth nor outward fair
12 Can make you live yourself in eyes of men.
    To give away yourself keeps yourself still,
    And you must live, drawn by your own sweet
        skill.

6 *unset* unplanted   8 *counterfeit* portrait   9 *lines of life* lineal
descendants   10 *time's pencil* artist of the present day   11 *fair*
beauty   13 *give away yourself* i.e., to beget children   13 *keeps*
preserves

17

Who will believe my verse in time to come
If it were filled with your most high deserts?
Though yet heaven knows it is but as a tomb
Which hides your life and shows not half your
    parts.   *4*
If I could write the beauty of your eyes,
And in fresh numbers number all your graces,
The age to come would say "This poet lies,
Such heavenly touches ne'er touched earthly faces." *8*
So should my papers, yellowed with their age,
Be scorned, like old men of less truth than tongue,
And your true rights be termed a poet's rage
And stretchèd meter of an antique song: *12*
    But were some child of yours alive that time,
    You should live twice, in it and in my rhyme.

2 *deserts* (rhymes with "parts")   4 *parts* good qualities   6 *numbers* verses   8 *touches* (1) strokes of pencil or brush (2) traits
11 *true rights* due praise   11 *rage* inspiration   12 *stretchèd meter* poetic exaggeration

18

Shall I compare thee to a summer's day?
Thou art more lovely and more temperate.
Rough winds do shake the darling buds of May,
4 And summer's lease hath all too short a date.
Sometime too hot the eye of heaven shines,
And often is his gold complexion dimmed;
And every fair from fair sometime declines,
8 By chance, or nature's changing course, untrimmed;
But thy eternal summer shall not fade,
Nor lose possession of that fair thou ow'st,
Nor shall Death brag thou wand'rest in his shade,
12 When in eternal lines to time thou grow'st.
    So long as men can breathe or eyes can see,
    So long lives this, and this gives life to thee.

4 *lease* allotted time   4 *date* duration   7 *fair from fair* beautiful
thing from beauty   8 *untrimmed* divested of ornament   10 *thou
ow'st* you possess

19

Devouring Time, blunt thou the lion's paws,
And make the earth devour her own sweet brood;
Pluck the keen teeth from the fierce tiger's jaws,
And burn the long-lived phoenix in her blood; 4
Make glad and sorry seasons as thou fleets,
And do whate'er thou wilt, swift-footed Time,
To the wide world and all her fading sweets;
But I forbid thee one most heinous crime, 8
O, carve not with thy hours my love's fair brow,
Nor draw no lines there with thine antique pen.
Him in thy course untainted do allow,
For beauty's pattern to succeeding men. 12
  Yet do thy worst, old Time; despite thy wrong,
  My love shall in my verse ever live young.

4 *phoenix* mythical bird that periodically is consumed in flames
and arises renewed (symbol of immortality)   4 *in her blood*
alive   10 *antique* (1) old (2) grotesque, antic   11 *untainted*
untouched

20

A woman's face, with Nature's own hand painted,
Hast thou, the master mistress of my passion;
A woman's gentle heart, but not acquainted
4 With shifting change, as is false women's fashion;
An eye more bright than theirs, less false in rolling,
Gilding the object whereupon it gazeth;
A man in hue all hues in his controlling,
Which steals men's eyes and women's souls
8   amazeth.
And for a woman wert thou first created,
Till Nature as she wrought thee fell a-doting,
And by addition me of thee defeated,
12 By adding one thing to my purpose nothing.
    But since she pricked thee out for women's
            pleasure,
    Mine be thy love, and thy love's use their
            treasure.

1 *Nature's* i.e., not Art's   2 *master mistress* supreme mistress
(some editors hyphenate, indicating that in this case the "mistress" is a "master")   2 *passion* love (or possibly love poems)
5 *rolling* i.e., roving from one to another   7 *hue* appearance
(both complexion and form)   11 *defeated* defrauded   13 *pricked
thee out* (1) marked you out (2) added a phallus (cf. line 12)

21

So is it not with me as with that Muse,
Stirred by a painted beauty to his verse,
Who heaven itself for ornament doth use,
And every fair with his fair doth rehearse;   *4*
Making a couplement of proud compare
With sun and moon, with earth and sea's rich gems,
With April's first-born flowers, and all things rare
That heaven's air in this huge rondure hems.   *8*
O, let me true in love but truly write,
And then believe me, my love is as fair
As any mother's child, though not so bright
As those gold candles fixed in heaven's air: *12*
    Let them say more that like of hearsay well;
    I will not praise that purpose not to sell.

1 *Muse* poet   2 *Stirred* inspired   4 *fair* beautiful thing   4 *rehearse* mention, i.e., compare   5 *couplement* combination   5 *compare* comparison   8 *rondure* sphere, world   8 *hems* encircles   13 *that like of hearsay well* who delight in empty talk   14 *that* who

22

My glass shall not persuade me I am old,
So long as youth and thou are of one date,
But when in thee Time's furrows I behold,
4   Then look I death my days should expiate.
For all that beauty that doth cover thee
Is but the seemly raiment of my heart,
Which in thy breast doth live, as thine in me.
8   How can I then be elder than thou art?
O, therefore, love, be of thyself so wary
As I, not for myself, but for thee will,
Bearing thy heart, which I will keep so chary
12   As tender nurse her babe from faring ill.
    Presume not on thy heart when mine is slain;
    Thou gav'st me thine, not to give back again.

2 *of one date* of the same age   4 *expiate* end   11 *chary* carefully   13 *Presume not on* do not lay claim to

23

As an unperfect actor on the stage,
Who with his fear is put besides his part,
Or some fierce thing replete with too much rage,
Whose strength's abundance weakens his own heart;   *4*
So I, for fear of trust, forget to say
The perfect ceremony of love's right,
And in mine own love's strength seem to decay,
O'ercharged with burden of mine own love's might.   *8*
O, let my books be then the eloquence
And dumb presagers of my speaking breast,
Who plead for love, and look for recompense,
More than that tongue that more hath more
        expressed.   *12*
    O, learn to read what silent love hath writ.
    To hear with eyes belongs to love's fine wit.

---

5 *for fear of trust* fearing to trust myself   **6** *right* (pun on "rite")
9 *books* (possibly it should be emended to "looks," i.e., though
silent, he hopes his looks will speak for him)   **10** *dumb presagers*
silent foretellers   **12** *more expressed* more often expressed
14 *wit* intelligence

24

Mine eye hath played the painter and hath steeled
Thy beauty's form in table of my heart;
My body is the frame wherein 'tis held,
4   And perspective it is best painter's art,
For through the painter must you see his skill,
To find where your true image pictured lies,
Which in my bosom's shop is hanging still,
8   That hath his windows glazèd with thine eyes.
Now see what good turns eyes for eyes have done:
Mine eyes have drawn thy shape, and thine for me
Are windows to my breast, wherethrough the sun
12 Delights to peep, to gaze therein on thee.
      Yet eyes this cunning want to grace their art,
      They draw but what they see, know not the heart.

1 *steeled* engraved   2 *table* tablet, picture   4 *perspective* (perhaps the idea is that the *frame*, in line 3, contributes to the perspective of the picture it encloses; some editors put a colon after *perspective*)   8 *his* its   8 *glazèd* covered as with glass   13 *cunning* ability   13 *want* lack

25

Let those who are in favor with their stars
Of public honor and proud titles boast,
Whilst I whom fortune of such triumph bars,
Unlooked for joy in that I honor most.   *4*
Great princes' favorites their fair leaves spread
But as the marigold at the sun's eye,
And in themselves their pride lies burièd,
For at a frown they in their glory die.   *8*
The painful warrior famousèd for might,
After a thousand victories once foiled,
Is from the book of honor rasèd quite,
And all the rest forgot for which he toiled.   *12*
    Then happy I that love and am beloved
    Where I may not remove, nor be removed.

---

4 *Unlooked for joy in that* unexpectedly enjoy that which   6 *But*
only   9 *painful* painstaking   11 *rasèd quite* erased entirely

26

Lord of my love, to whom in vassalage
Thy merit hath my duty strongly knit,
To thee I send this written ambassage,
4   To witness duty, not to show my wit.
Duty so great, which wit so poor as mine
May make seem bare, in wanting words to show it,
But that I hope some good conceit of thine
8   In thy soul's thought, all naked, will bestow it;
Till whatsoever star that guides my moving
Points on me graciously with fair aspect,
And puts apparel on my tottered loving
12   To show me worthy of thy sweet respect.
      Then may I dare to boast how I do love thee;
      Till then, not show my head where thou mayst
          prove me.

3 *written ambassage* message   4 *wit* mental powers   6 *wanting*
lacking   7 *conceit* thought   8 *all naked, will bestow it* will ac-
cept (give lodging to) my bare statement   9 *moving* life
10 *aspect* astrological influence   11 *tottered* tattered   14 *prove*
test

27

Weary with toil, I haste me to my bed,
The dear repose for limbs with travel tired,
But then begins a journey in my head
To work my mind when body's work's expired;   *4*
For then my thoughts, from far where I abide,
Intend a zealous pilgrimage to thee,
And keep my drooping eyelids open wide,
Looking on darkness which the blind do see;   *8*
Save that my soul's imaginary sight
Presents thy shadow to my sightless view,
Which like a jewel hung in ghastly night,
Makes black night beauteous and her old face new.   *12*
   Lo, thus, by day my limbs, by night my mind,
   For thee, and for myself, no quiet find.

2 *travel* (1) labor (2) journeying   4 *To work* to set at work
6 *Intend* set out upon   9 *imaginary* imaginative   10 *shadow*
image

28

How can I then return in happy plight
That am debarred the benefit of rest,
When day's oppression is not eased by night,
4 But day by night and night by day oppressed,
And each, though enemies to either's reign,
Do in consent shake hands to torture me,
The one by toil, the other to complain
8 How far I toil, still farther off from thee?
I tell the day, to please him, thou art bright
And dost him grace when clouds do blot the heaven;
So flatter I the swart-complexioned night,
12 When sparkling stars twire not, thou gild'st the even.
But day doth daily draw my sorrows longer,
And night doth nightly make grief's length seem
stronger.

6 *shake hands* unite   7 *the other to complain* i.e., the night causes me to complain   10 *dost him grace* i.e., shine for him   11 *swart-complexioned* dark complexioned   12 *twire* twinkle (?)   12 *thou gild'st the even* you brighten the evening

29

When, in disgrace with Fortune and men's eyes,
I all alone beweep my outcast state,
And trouble deaf heaven with my bootless cries,
And look upon myself and curse my fate,   *4*
Wishing me like to one more rich in hope,
Featured like him, like him with friends possessed,
Desiring this man's art, and that man's scope,
With what I most enjoy contented least;   *8*
Yet in these thoughts myself almost despising,
Haply I think on thee, and then my state,
Like to the lark at break of day arising
From sullen earth, sings hymns at heaven's gate;   *12*
    For thy sweet love rememb'red such wealth
        brings,
    That then I scorn to change my state with kings.

1 *disgrace* disfavor   3 *bootless* useless   6 *like him, like him* like
a second man, like a third man   7 *art* skill   7 *scope* mental
power   10 *Haply* perchance   10 *state* i.e., condition   12 *sullen*
gloomy

30

When to the sessions of sweet silent thought
I summon up remembrance of things past,
I sigh the lack of many a thing I sought,
4 And with old woes new wail my dear Time's waste.
Then can I drown an eye, unused to flow,
For precious friends hid in death's dateless night,
And weep afresh love's long since canceled woe,
8 And moan th' expense of many a vanished sight;
Then can I grieve at grievances foregone,
And heavily from woe to woe tell o'er
The sad account of fore-bemoanèd moan,
12 Which I new pay as if not paid before.
    But if the while I think on thee, dear friend,
    All losses are restored and sorrows end.

1 *sessions* sittings of a court or council   4 *new wail* newly bewail
4 *my dear Time's waste* Time's destruction of things dear to me
6 *dateless* endless   7 *canceled* i.e., because paid in full   8 *expense* loss   9 *foregone* former   10 *tell* count

31

Thy bosom is endearèd with all hearts
Which I by lacking have supposèd dead;
And there reigns love and all love's loving parts,
And all those friends which I thought burièd.   *4*
How many a holy and obsequious tear
Hath dear religious love stol'n from mine eye,
As interest of the dead, which now appear
But things removed that hidden in there lie.   *8*
Thou art the grave where buried love doth live,
Hung with the trophies of my lovers gone,
Who all their parts of me to thee did give;
That due of many now is thine alone.   *12*
　　Their images I loved I view in thee,
　　And thou, all they, hast all the all of me.

---

1 *endearèd* made more precious 5 *obsequious* funereal 6 *religious* worshipful 7 *interest* right 7 *which* who 10 *trophies* memorials 11 *parts* shares 12 *That due of many* that which was due to many

32

If thou survive my well-contented day,
When that churl Death my bones with dust shall
     cover,
And shalt by fortune once more resurvey
4   These poor rude lines of thy deceasèd lover,
Compare them with the bett'ring of the time,
And though they be outstripped by every pen,
Reserve them for my love, not for their rhyme,
8   Exceeded by the height of happier men.
O, then vouchsafe me but this loving thought:
"Had my friend's Muse grown with this growing age,
A dearer birth than this his love had brought,
12 To march in ranks of better equipage;
     But since he died, and poets better prove,
     Theirs for their style I'll read, his for his love."

1 *my well-contented day* i.e., my day of death whose arrival
will content me   5 *bett'ring* improved poetry   7 *Reserve* pre-
serve   8 *happier* more gifted   12 *of better equipage* better
equipped

33

Full many a glorious morning have I seen
Flatter the mountain tops with sovereign eye,
Kissing with golden face the meadows green,
Gilding pale streams with heavenly alchemy;   *4*
Anon permit the basest clouds to ride
With ugly rack on his celestial face,
And from the forlorn world his visage hide,
Stealing unseen to west with this disgrace.   *8*
Even so my sun one early morn did shine,
With all triumphant splendor on my brow;
But out alack, he was but one hour mine,
The region cloud hath masked him from me now.   *12*
   Yet him for this my love no whit disdaineth;
   Suns of the world may stain when heaven's sun
      staineth.

---

2 *Flatter . . . eye* i.e., the sun, like a monarch's eye, flatters all
that it rests upon 5 *Anon* soon 5 *basest* darkest 6 *rack*
vapory clouds 7 *forlorn* forsaken 11 *out alack* alas 12 *re-
gion cloud* clouds of the upper air 14 *stain* grow dim

34

Why didst thou promise such a beauteous day,
And make me travel forth without my cloak,
To let base clouds o'ertake me in my way,
4   Hiding thy brav'ry in their rotten smoke?
'Tis not enough that through the cloud thou break,
To dry the rain on my storm-beaten face,
For no man well of such a salve can speak,
8   That heals the wound, and cures not the disgrace.
Nor can thy shame give physic to my grief;
Though thou repent, yet I have still the loss.
Th' offender's sorrow lends but weak relief
12 To him that bears the strong offense's cross.
 Ah, but those tears are pearl which thy love
   sheeds,
 And they are rich and ransom all ill deeds.

3 *base* dark 4 *brav'ry* finery 4 *rotten smoke* unwholesome
vapors 9 *physic* remedy 13 *sheeds* sheds 14 *ransom* atone
for

35

No more be grieved at that which thou hast done:
Roses have thorns, and silver fountains mud,
Clouds and eclipses stain both moon and sun,
And loathsome canker lives in sweetest bud.   *4*
All men make faults, and even I in this,
Authorizing thy trespass with compare,
Myself corrupting, salving thy amiss,
Excusing thy sins more than thy sins are;   *8*
For to thy sensual fault I bring in sense—
Thy adverse party is thy advocate—
And 'gainst myself a lawful plea commence.
Such civil war is in my love and hate   *12*
    That I an accessory needs must be
    To that sweet thief which sourly robs from me.

3 *stain* darken   4 *canker* cankerworm (that destroys flowers)
6 *Authorizing* justifying   6 *with compare* by comparison   7
salving thy amiss palliating your misbehavior   8 *Excusing . . .
are* i.e., offering excuses more abundant than your sins (?)
9 *to thy . . . sense* perhaps: to your physical fault I add reason
("sense"); possibly, however, "in sense" is a pun on "incense,"
i.e., my reason sweetens your sins   13 *accessory* accomplice
14 *sourly* bitterly

36

Let me confess that we two must be twain,
Although our undivided loves are one.
So shall those blots that do with me remain,
4　Without thy help, by me be borne alone.
In our two loves there is but one respect,
Though in our lives a separable spite,
Which though it alter not love's sole effect,
8　Yet doth it steal sweet hours from love's delight.
I may not evermore acknowledge thee,
Lest my bewailèd guilt should do thee shame;
Nor thou with public kindness honor me,
12　Unless thou take that honor from thy name.
　　But do not so; I love thee in such sort
　　As, thou being mine, mine is thy good report.

5 *but one respect* only one regard　6 *separable spite* spiteful
separation　7 *sole* unique　13–14 *But do . . . report* (this coup-
let is repeated in Sonnet 96)　14 *report* reputation

37

As a decrepit father takes delight
To see his active child do deeds of youth,
So I, made lame by Fortune's dearest spite,
Take all my comfort of thy worth and truth.   *4*
For whether beauty, birth, or wealth, or wit,
Or any of these all, or all, or more,
Entitled in their parts do crownèd sit,
I make my love engrafted to this store.   *8*
So then I am not lame, poor, nor despised
Whilst that this shadow doth such substance give
That I in thy abundance am sufficed
And by a part of all thy glory live.   *12*
    Look what is best, that best I wish in thee.
    This wish I have, then ten times happy me!

3 *dearest* most grievous 4 *of* from 5 *wit* intelligence 7 *Entitled in . . . sit* sit as king entitled to their places 8 *engrafted to this store* i.e., fused with and nourished by this abundance 13 *Look what* whatever

38

How can my Muse want subject to invent,
While thou dost breathe, that pour'st into my verse
Thine own sweet argument, too excellent
4   For every vulgar paper to rehearse?
O, give thyself the thanks, if aught in me
Worthy perusal stand against thy sight;
For who's so dumb that cannot write to thee
8   When thou thyself dost give invention light?
Be thou the tenth Muse, ten times more in worth
Than those old nine which rhymers invocate;
And he that calls on thee, let him bring forth
12   Eternal numbers to outlive long date.
    If my slight Muse do please these curious days,
    The pain be mine, but thine shall be the praise.

1 *want subject to invent* lack subject matter for creation   2 *that* who   3 *argument* subject   4 *vulgar paper* ordinary composition 4 *rehearse* repeat   5 *in me* of my writings   6 *stand against thy sight* meet your eyes, i.e., be written for you   7 *dumb* mute 8 *invention* imagination   10 *invocate* invoke   12 *numbers* verses 12 *long date* a distant era   13 *curious* critical   14 *pain* trouble

39

O, how thy worth with manners may I sing,
When thou art all the better part of me?
What can mine own praise to mine own self bring,
And what is't but mine own when I praise thee?   *4*
Even for this, let us divided live,
And our dear love lose name of single one,
That by this separation I may give
That due to thee which thou deserv'st alone.   *8*
O, absence, what a torment wouldst thou prove,
Were it not thy sour leisure gave sweet leave
To entertain the time with thoughts of love,
Which time and thoughts so sweetly dost deceive,   *12*
    And that thou teachest how to make one twain
    By praising him here who doth hence remain.

1 *with manners* i.e., without self-praise   5 *for* because of   11 *entertain* pass

40

Take all my loves, my love, yea take them all;
What hast thou then more than thou hadst before?
No love, my love, that thou mayst true love call;
4 All mine was thine, before thou hadst this more.
Then if for my love thou my love receivest,
I cannot blame thee for my love thou usest;
But yet be blamed, if thou this self deceivest
8 By willful taste of what thyself refusest.
I do forgive thy robb'ry, gentle thief,
Although thou steal thee all my poverty;
And yet love knows it is a greater grief
12 To bear love's wrong than hate's known injury.
    Lascivious grace, in whom all ill well shows,
    Kill me with spites; yet we must not be foes.

6 *for* because 6 *thou usest* you are intimate with 7 *this self* i.e., your other self, the poet ("this self" is, however, often emended to "thy self") 8 *willful taste* capricious enjoyment 10 *my poverty* the little I have 12 *known* open 13 *Lascivious grace* i.e., you who have such grace even when lascivious

41

Those pretty wrongs that liberty commits,
When I am sometime absent from thy heart,
Thy beauty and thy years full well befits,
For still temptation follows where thou art.   *4*
Gentle thou art, and therefore to be won;
Beauteous thou art, therefore to be assailed;
And when a woman woos, what woman's son
Will sourly leave her till she have prevailed?   *8*
Ay me, but yet thou might'st my seat forbear,
And chide thy beauty and thy straying youth,
Who lead thee in their riot even there
Where thou art forced to break a twofold truth: *12*
  Hers, by thy beauty tempting her to thee,
  Thine, by thy beauty being false to me.

1 *pretty* petty (?)   1 *liberty* licentiousness   4 *still* always
9 *seat* place   11 *Who* which   11 *riot* revels   12 *truth* duty

42

That thou hast her, it is not all my grief,
And yet it may be said I loved her dearly;
That she hath thee is of my wailing chief,
4   A loss in love that touches me more nearly.
Loving offenders, thus I will excuse ye:
Thou dost love her, because thou know'st I love her,
And for my sake even so doth she abuse me,
8   Suff'ring my friend for my sake to approve her.
If I lose thee, my loss is my love's gain,
And losing her, my friend hath found that loss:
Both find each other, and I lose both twain,
12   And both for my sake lay on me this cross.
        But here's the joy: my friend and I are one;
        Sweet flattery! Then she loves but me alone.

3 *of my wailing chief* chief cause of my grief   4 *nearly* closely
7 *abuse* deceive   8 *approve* test, experience sensually   9 *love's*
mistress'

43

When most I wink, then do mine eyes best see,
For all the day they view things unrespected,
But when I sleep, in dreams they look on thee
And, darkly bright, are bright in dark directed.   *4*
Then thou, whose shadow shadows doth make
    bright,
How would thy shadow's form form happy show
To the clear day with thy much clearer light,
When to unseeing eyes thy shade shines so!   *8*
How would, I say, mine eyes be blessèd made,
By looking on thee in the living day,
When in dead night thy fair imperfect shade
Through heavy sleep on sightless eyes doth stay!   *12*
    All days are nights to see till I see thee,
      And nights bright days when dreams do show thee
      me.

1 *I wink* I close my eyes, i.e., I sleep 2 *unrespected* unregarded
5 *shadow shadows* image darkness 6 *thy shadow's form* the
body that casts your shadow 13 *are nights to see* look like
nights

44

If the dull substance of my flesh were thought,
Injurious distance should not stop my way,
For then despite of space I would be brought,
4　From limits far remote, where thou dost stay.
No matter then although my foot did stand
Upon the farthest earth removed from thee;
For nimble thought can jump both sea and land,
8　As soon as think the place where he would be.
But, ah, thought kills me that I am not thought,
To leap large lengths of miles when thou art gone,
But that so much of earth and water wrought,
12　I must attend time's leisure with my moan,
　　Receiving naught by elements so slow
　　But heavy tears, badges of either's woe.

1 *dull substance* i.e., earth and water (in contrast to air and fire)
2 *Injurious* malicious　4 *limits* districts　4 *where* to where
6 *farthest earth removed* earth farthest removed　8 *he* it
11 *wrought* compounded　12 *attend* await　14 *badges of either's
woe* i.e., earth's because heavy, water's because wet (and perhaps
because salty)

45

The other two, slight air and purging fire,
Are both with thee, wherever I abide;
The first my thought, the other my desire,
These present-absent with swift motion slide.   *4*
For when these quicker elements are gone
In tender embassy of love to thee,
My life, being made of four, with two alone
Sinks down to death, oppressed with melancholy;   *8*
Until life's composition be recured
By those swift messengers returned from thee,
Who even but now come back again, assured
Of thy fair health, recounting it to me.   *12*
   This told, I joy, but then no longer glad,
   I send them back again, and straight grow sad.

1 *two* i.e., of the four elements (see note on the first line of the
previous sonnet)   1 *slight* insubstantial   4 *present-absent* now
here, now gone   7 *two alone* i.e., earth and water   9 *recured*
restored to health   10 *messengers* i.e., fire and air

46

Mine eye and heart are at a mortal war
How to divide the conquest of thy sight;
Mine eye my heart thy picture's sight would bar,
4   My heart mine eye the freedom of that right.
My heart doth plead that thou in him dost lie—
A closet never pierced with crystal eyes;
But the defendant doth that plea deny,
8   And says in him thy fair appearance lies.
To 'cide this title is impanelèd
A quest of thoughts, all tenants to the heart;
And by their verdict is determinèd
12   The clear eye's moiety, and the dear heart's part:
    As thus—mine eye's due is thy outward part,
    And my heart's right thy inward love of heart.

2 *conquest of thy sight* i.e., the right to gaze on you   10 *quest*
inquest, jury   12 *moiety* portion

47

Betwixt mine eye and heart a league is took,
And each doth good turns now unto the other.
When that mine eye is famished for a look,
Or heart in love with sighs himself doth smother, 4
With my love's picture then my eye doth feast,
And to the painted banquet bids my heart.
Another time mine eye is my heart's guest
And in his thoughts of love doth share a part. 8
So, either by thy picture or my love,
Thyself away are present still with me;
For thou not farther than my thoughts canst move,
And I am still with them, and they with thee; 12
   Or, if they sleep, thy picture in my sight
   Awakes my heart to heart's and eye's delight.

1 *a league is took* an agreement is made   8 *his* i.e., the heart's
12 *still* always

48

How careful was I, when I took my way,
Each trifle under truest bars to thrust,
That to my use it might unusèd stay
4   From hands of falsehood, in sure wards of trust!
But thou, to whom my jewels trifles are,
Most worthy comfort, now my greatest grief,
Thou best of dearest, and mine only care,
8   Art left the prey of every vulgar thief.
Thee have I not locked up in any chest,
Save where thou art not, though I feel thou art,
Within the gentle closure of my breast,
12   From whence at pleasure thou mayst come and part;
     And even thence thou wilt be stol'n, I fear,
     For truth proves thievish for a prize so dear.

2 *trifle* i.e., in comparison with the person addressed   2 *truest*
most trusty   4 *wards* cells   5 *to* in comparison with   8 *vulgar*
common   9 *chest* (1) coffer (2) breast   14 *truth* honesty

49

Against that time, if ever that time come,
When I shall see thee frown on my defects,
Whenas thy love hath cast his utmost sum,
Called to that audit by advised respects;   4
Against that time when thou shalt strangely pass,
And scarcely greet me with that sun, thine eye,
When love, converted from the thing it was,
Shall reasons find of settled gravity.   8
Against that time do I ensconce me here
Within the knowledge of mine own desart,
And this my hand against myself uprear,
To guard the lawful reasons on thy part.   12
   To leave poor me thou hast the strength of laws,
   Since why to love I can allege no cause.

---

1 *Against* in preparation for   3 *cast his utmost sum* computed
its final reckoning   4 *advised respects* well-considered reasons
5 *strangely* with a reserved manner (like a stranger) 9 *ensconce
me* fortify myself   10 *desart* desert   11 *uprear* raise as a witness

50

How heavy do I journey on the way
When what I seek, my weary travel's end,
Doth teach that ease and that repose to say,
4 "Thus far the miles are measured from thy friend."
The beast that bears me, tired with my woe,
Plods dully on, to bear that weight in me,
As if by some instinct the wretch did know
8 His rider loved not speed, being made from thee.
The bloody spur cannot provoke him on,
That sometimes anger thrusts into his hide,
Which heavily he answers with a groan,
12 More sharp to me than spurring to his side;
     For that same groan doth put this in my mind:
     My grief lies onward and my joy behind.

1 *heavy* sadly

51

Thus can my love excuse the slow offense
Of my dull bearer, when from thee I speed:
From where thou art why should I haste me thence?
Till I return, of posting is no need.   *4*
O, what excuse will my poor beast then find
When swift extremity can seem but slow?
Then should I spur, though mounted on the wind,
In wingèd speed no motion shall I know.   *8*
Then can no horse with my desire keep pace;
Therefore desire, of perfect'st love being made,
Shall neigh, no dull flesh in his fiery race;
But love, for love, thus shall excuse my jade: *12*
    Since from thee going he went willful slow,
    Towards thee I'll run and give him leave to go.

1 *slow offense* offense of slowness   4 *posting* riding hastily
6 *swift extremity* extreme swiftness   11 *neigh* i.e., in exultation in
its ethereal speed (?) (some editors emend to "weigh" with the
meaning that desire refuses to keep to the slow pace of the
horse and will not weigh down the horse's "dull flesh")   12 *jade*
nag   14 *go* walk

52

So am I as the rich, whose blessèd key
Can bring him to his sweet up-lockèd treasure,
The which he will not ev'ry hour survey,
4   For blunting the fine point of seldom pleasure.
Therefore are feasts so solemn and so rare,
Since, seldom coming, in the long year set,
Like stones of worth they thinly placèd are,
8   Or captain jewels in the carcanet.
So is the time that keeps you as my chest,
Or as the wardrobe which the robe doth hide,
To make some special instant special blest,
12   By new unfolding his imprisoned pride.
     Blessèd are you whose worthiness gives scope,
     Being had, to triumph, being lacked, to hope.

1 *key* (rhymes with "survey")   4 *For* for fear of   4 *seldom pleasure* pleasure infrequently enjoyed   8 *captain* chief   8 *carcanet* collar of jewels   12 *his* its

53

What is your substance, whereof are you made,
That millions of strange shadows on you tend?
Since everyone hath, every one, one shade,
And you, but one, can every shadow lend.   *4*
Describe Adonis, and the counterfeit
Is poorly imitated after you;
On Helen's cheek all art of beauty set,
And you in Grecian tires are painted new.   *8*
Speak of the spring and foison of the year;
The one doth shadow of your beauty show,
The other as your bounty doth appear,
And you in every blessèd shape we know.   *12*
    In all external grace you have some part,
    But you like none, none you, for constant heart.

2 *strange shadows* images not your own (the images of Adonis, Helen, spring, and autumn in the following lines)   2 *tend* wait on   3 *shade* shadow   4 *And you . . . lend* i.e., and you, though one, can provide a variety of good traits (?)   5 *counterfeit* picture   8 *tires* attire   9 *foison* rich harvest

54

O, how much more doth beauty beauteous seem,
By that sweet ornament which truth doth give!
The rose looks fair, but fairer we it deem
4 For that sweet odor which doth in it live.
The canker blooms have full as deep a dye,
As the perfumèd tincture of the roses,
Hang on such thorns, and play as wantonly,
8 When summer's breath their maskèd buds discloses;
But, for their virtue only is their show,
They live unwooed and unrespected fade,
Die to themselves. Sweet roses do not so;
12 Of their sweet deaths are sweetest odors made.
    And so of you, beauteous and lovely youth,
    When that shall vade, by verse distills your truth.

2 *truth* fidelity   5 *canker blooms* dog roses (which lack the perfume of the damask rose)   6 *tincture* color   7 *wantonly* unrestrainedly   8 *maskèd* hidden   8 *discloses* opens   9 *for* because   9 *virtue only* only merit   10 *unrespected* unregarded   12 *are sweetest odors made* perfumes are made   14 *vade* depart, perish   14 *by verse distills your truth* by means of verse your essence is distilled ("by" is often emended to "my")

55

Not marble, nor the gilded monuments
Of princes, shall outlive this pow'rful rhyme,
But you shall shine more bright in these contents
Than unswept stone, besmeared with sluttish time.   *4*
When wasteful war shall statues overturn,
And broils root out the work of masonry,
Nor Mars his sword nor war's quick fire shall burn
The living record of your memory.   *8*
'Gainst death and all oblivious enmity
Shall you pace forth; your praise shall still find room
Even in the eyes of all posterity
That wear this world out to the ending doom.   *12*
   So, till the judgment that yourself arise,
    You live in this, and dwell in lovers' eyes.

---

3 *these contents* i.e., the contents of this poem   4 *Than* than in
4 *stone* memorial tablet in the floor of a church   6 *broils* skir-
mishes   7 *Nor . . . nor* neither . . . nor   7 *Mars his sword* Mars'
sword   7 *burn* (either metaphorically governs "Mars his sword"
as well as "war's quick fire," or the verb governing "Mars his
sword" is omitted)   9 *all oblivious enmity* all enmity that brings
oblivion (?) enmity that brings oblivion to all (?)   12 *wear this
world out* outlasts this world   13 *judgment that* Judgment Day
when   14 *lovers'* admirers'

56

Sweet love, renew thy force; be it not said
Thy edge should blunter be than appetite,
Which but today by feeding is allayed,
4 Tomorrow sharp'ned in his former might.
So, love, be thou; although today thou fill
Thy hungry eyes even till they wink with fullness,
Tomorrow see again, and do not kill
8 The spirit of love with a perpetual dullness.
Let this sad int'rim like the ocean be
Which parts the shore where two contracted new
Come daily to the banks, that, when they see
12 Return of love, more blest may be the view;
 Or call it winter, which being full of care,
  Makes summer's welcome thrice more wished,
   more rare.

1 *love* spirit of love, i.e., not the beloved   2 *edge* keenness
2 *appetite* lust   6 *wink* shut in sleep   9 *sad int'rim* period of
estrangement (?)   10 *contracted new* newly betrothed

57

Being your slave, what should I do but tend
Upon the hours and times of your desire?
I have no precious time at all to spend,
Nor services to do till you require.   4
Nor dare I chide the world-without-end hour
Whilst I, my sovereign, watch the clock for you,
Nor think the bitterness of absence sour
When you have bid your servant once adieu.   8
Nor dare I question with my jealous thought
Where you may be, or your affairs suppose,
But, like a sad slave, stay and think of naught
Save where you are how happy you make those.   12
    So true a fool is love that in your will,
    Though you do anything, he thinks no ill.

1 *tend* wait 5 *world-without-end* seemingly endless 7 *Nor think* nor dare I think 9 *question* dispute 10 *suppose* guess at 13 *will* desire (with a pun on Shakespeare's first name)

58

That god forbid that made me first your slave
I should in thought control your times of pleasure,
Or at your hand th' account of hours to crave,
4   Being your vassal bound to stay your leisure.
O, let me suffer, being at your beck,
Th' imprisoned absence of your liberty;
And patience, tame to sufferance, bide each check,
8   Without accusing you of injury.
Be where you list, your charter is so strong
That you yourself may privilege your time
To what you will; to you it doth belong
12   Yourself to pardon of self-doing crime.
      I am to wait, though waiting so be hell,
      Not blame your pleasure, be it ill or well.

4 *stay your leisure* wait until you are unoccupied   6 *Th' im-prisoned . . . liberty* the imprisonment brought to me by your freedom to absent yourself   7 *And patience . . . check* i.e., and patience, disciplined to accept suffering, endures every rebuke 8 *injury* injustice   9 *list* wish   9 *charter* privilege   10 *privilege* authorize   12 *self-doing* (1) done by one's self (2) done to one's self   13 *am to* must

59

If there be nothing new, but that which is
Hath been before, how are our brains beguiled,
Which, laboring for invention, bear amiss
The second burden of a former child!   4
O, that record could with a backward look,
Even of five hundred courses of the sun,
Show me your image in some antique book,
Since mind at first in character was done;   8
That I might see what the old world could say
To this composèd wonder of your frame;
Whether we are mended, or whe'r better they,
Or whether revolution be the same.   12
   O, sure I am the wits of former days
   To subjects worse have given admiring praise.

3 *for invention* i.e., to create something new   3–4 *bear . . .
former child* futilely bring forth only a reproduction of what had
already been created   5 *record* memory   6 *courses of the sun*
years   8 *Since mind . . . done* since thought was first expressed
in writing   10 *composèd wonder* wonderful composition   11
mended bettered   11 *whe'r* whether   12 *revolution be the same*
i.e., cycles are repeated   13 *wits* men of intellect

60

Like as the waves make towards the pebbled shore,
So do our minutes hasten to their end;
Each changing place with that which goes before,
4   In sequent toil all forwards do contend.
Nativity, once in the main of light,
Crawls to maturity, wherewith being crowned,
Crooked eclipses 'gainst his glory fight,
8   And Time that gave doth now his gift confound.
Time doth transfix the flourish set on youth,
And delves the parallels in beauty's brow,
Feeds on the rarities of nature's truth,
12   And nothing stands but for his scythe to mow:
        And yet to times in hope my verse shall stand,
        Praising thy worth, despite his cruel hand.

4 *sequent* successive   5 *Nativity . . . light* i.e., the newborn, at
first in the ocean (metaphorical for "great expanse" or "flood")
of light   7 *Crooked* malignant   8 *confound* destroy   9 *transfix*
destroy   10 *delves the parallels* i.e., digs wrinkles   13 *times in
hope* future times

61

Is it thy will thy image should keep open
My heavy eyelids to the weary night?
Dost thou desire my slumbers should be broken
While shadows like to thee do mock my sight?   4
Is it thy spirit that thou send'st from thee
So far from home into my deeds to pry,
To find out shames and idle hours in me,
The scope and tenure of thy jealousy?   8
O no, thy love, though much, is not so great.
It is my love that keeps mine eye awake,
Mine own true love that doth my rest defeat,
To play the watchman ever for thy sake.   12
    For thee watch I, whilst thou dost wake elsewhere,
    From me far off, with others all too near.

---

4 *shadows* images   8 *The scope . . . jealousy* the aim and mean-
ing of your suspicion   11 *defeat* destroy   13 *watch* keep awake
13 *wake* revel at night (with a pun on "wake up in bed")

62

Sin of self-love possesseth all mine eye
And all my soul and all my every part;
And for this sin there is no remedy,
4   It is so grounded inward in my heart.
Methinks no face so gracious is as mine,
No shape so true, no truth of such account,
And for myself mine own worth do define,
8   As I all other in all worths surmount.
But when my glass shows me myself indeed,
Beated and chopped with tanned antiquity,
Mine own self-love quite contrary I read;
12   Self so self-loving were iniquity.
    'Tis thee, myself, that for myself I praise,
    Painting my age with beauty of thy days.

---

5 *gracious* attractive   8 *As* as though   8 *other* others   10 *chopped* creased   10 *antiquity* old age   13 *myself* my alter ego   13 *that for* whom as   14 *days* i.e., youth

63

Against my love shall be as I am now,
With Time's injurious hand crushed and o'erworn;
When hours have drained his blood and filled his
    brow
With lines and wrinkles, when his youthful morn   *4*
Hath traveled on to Age's steepy night,
And all those beauties whereof now he's king
Are vanishing, or vanished out of sight,
Stealing away the treasure of his spring;   *8*
For such a time do I now fortify
Against confounding Age's cruel knife,
That he shall never cut from memory
My sweet love's beauty, though my lover's life.   *12*
  His beauty shall in these black lines be seen,
  And they shall live, and he in them still green.

1 *Against* in expectation of the time when   5 *Age's steepy night*
i.e., old age, which precipitously leads to the darkness of death
9 *fortify* build defenses   10 *confounding* destructive   10 *knife*
i.e., Time's scythe   12 *my lover's life* (1) the life of my lover (2)
the life of me, the lover

64

When I have seen by Time's fell hand defaced
The rich proud cost of outworn buried age,
When sometime lofty towers I see down-razed,
4   And brass eternal slave to mortal rage;
When I have seen the hungry ocean gain
Advantage on the kingdom of the shore,
And the firm soil win of the wat'ry main,
8   Increasing store with loss and loss with store;
When I have seen such interchange of state,
Or state itself confounded to decay,
Ruin hath taught me thus to ruminate,
12   That Time will come and take my love away.
      This thought is as a death, which cannot choose
      But weep to have that which it fears to lose.

1 *fell* cruel   2 *cost* splendor   2 *age* past times   3 *sometime* once
4 *brass eternal* everlasting brass   4 *mortal rage* the rage of
mortality   6 *Advantage* i.e., inroads   8 *Increasing store . . .
store* i.e., now one increases in abundance (*store*) with the other's
loss, now one repairs its loss with abundance taken from the
other   9 *state* condition (but in line 10 *state* = greatness)
10 *confounded* destroyed   14 *to have* because it has

65

Since brass, nor stone, nor earth, nor boundless sea,
But sad mortality o'ersways their power,
How with this rage shall beauty hold a plea,
Whose action is no stronger than a flower?   *4*
O, how shall summer's honey breath hold out
Against the wrackful siege of batt'ring days,
When rocks impregnable are not so stout,
Nor gates of steel so strong but Time decays?   *8*
O, fearful meditation, where, alack,
Shall Time's best jewel from Time's chest lie hid?
Or what strong hand can hold his swift foot back,
Or who his spoil of beauty can forbid?   *12*
   O, none, unless this miracle have might,
   That in black ink my love may still shine bright.

1 *Since* since there is neither   3 *rage* fury   3 *hold* maintain
4 *action* case, suit   6 *wrackful* destructive   8 *decays* causes
them to decay   10 *from Time's chest lie hid* i.e., conceal itself
to avoid being enclosed in Time's coffer   12 *spoil* plundering
14 *my love* my beloved

66

Tired with all these, for restful death I cry,
As, to behold desert a beggar born,
And needy nothing trimmed in jollity,
4   And purest faith unhappily forsworn,
And gilded honor shamefully misplaced,
And maiden virtue rudely strumpeted,
And right perfection wrongfully disgraced,
8   And strength by limping sway disabled,
And art made tongue-tied by authority,
And folly (doctorlike) controlling skill,
And simple truth miscalled simplicity,
12   And captive good attending captain ill.
     Tired with all these, from these would I be gone,
     Save that to die, I leave my love alone.

2 *As* for instance   2 *desert* a deserving person   3 *needy . . . jollity* i.e., a nonentity, who is poor in virtues, festively attired   4 *unhappily forsworn* miserably perjured   5 *gilded* golden   7 *disgraced* disfigured   8 *limping sway* i.e., incompetent authority   10 *doctorlike* with the air of a learned man   11 *simple* pure   11 *simplicity* stupidity   12 *attending* subordinated to

67

Ah, wherefore with infection should he live,
And with his presence grace impiety,
That sin by him advantage should achieve
And lace itself with his society?   *4*
Why should false painting imitate his cheek
And steal dead seeing of his living hue?
Why should poor beauty indirectly seek
Roses of shadow, since his rose is true?   *8*
Why should he live, now Nature bankrout is,
Beggared of blood to blush through lively veins,
For she hath no exchequer now but his,
And, proud of many, lives upon his gains?   *12*
  O, him she stores, to show what wealth she had,
  In days long since, before these last so bad.

---

1 *infection* an age of corruption   4 *lace* adorn   5 *false painting*
(possibly the reference is to the use of cosmetics or possibly to
portraiture)   6 *dead seeing* the lifeless appearance (though per-
haps *seeing* should be emended to "seeming")   7 *poor* second-
rate   7 *indirectly* by imitation   8 *of shadow* painted (?)   9 *bank-
rout* bankrupt   10 *Beggared . . . veins* i.e., so impoverished
that it can blush only with the aid of cosmetics   11 *exchequer*
treasury (of natural beauty)   12 *proud* (perhaps "falsely
proud," but possibly should be emended to " 'prived," i.e., de-
prived)

68

Thus is his cheek the map of days outworn,
When beauty lived and died as flowers do now,
Before these bastard signs of fair were born,
4   Or durst inhabit on a living brow;
Before the golden tresses of the dead,
The right of sepulchers, were shorn away
To live a second life on second head,
8   Ere beauty's dead fleece made another gay.
In him those holy antique hours are seen,
Without all ornament, itself and true,
Making no summer of another's green,
12   Robbing no old to dress his beauty new;
     And him as for a map doth Nature store,
     To show false Art what beauty was of yore.

1 *map* representation, picture   1 *days outworn* past times   3
bastard signs of fair false appearances (cosmetics, wigs) of beauty
3 *born* (with pun on "borne")   9 *antique hours* ancient times
10 *all* any   13 *store* preserve

69

Those parts of thee that the world's eye doth view
Want nothing that the thought of hearts can mend;
All tongues, the voice of souls, give thee that due,
Utt'ring bare truth, even so as foes commend.   4
Thy outward thus with outward praise is crowned,
But those same tongues that give thee so thine own
In other accents do this praise confound
By seeing farther than the eye hath shown.   8
They look into the beauty of thy mind,
And that in guess they measure by thy deeds;
Then, churls, their thoughts, although their eyes
     were kind,
To thy fair flower add the rank smell of weeds;   12
   But why thy odor matcheth not thy show,
   The soil is this, that thou dost common grow.

1 *parts* outward qualities   2 *Want* lack   4 *even so as foes com-*
mend i.e., without exaggeration   6 *so thine own* i.e., your due
7 *confound* destroy   14 *soil* (1) ground (2) blemish

70

That thou art blamed shall not be thy defect,
For slander's mark was ever yet the fair;
The ornament of beauty is suspect,
4   A crow that flies in heaven's sweetest air.
So thou be good, slander doth but approve
Thy worth the greater, being wooed of time;
For canker vice the sweetest buds doth love,
8   And thou present'st a pure unstainèd prime.
Thou hast passed by the ambush of young days,
Either not assailed, or victor being charged;
Yet this thy praise cannot be so thy praise
12   To tie up envy, evermore enlarged.
    If some suspect of ill masked not thy show,
    Then thou alone kingdoms of hearts shouldst owe.

3 *The ornament of beauty is suspect* suspicion (because it always seeks out the beautiful) is an ornament of beauty   5 *So* provided that   5 *approve* prove   6 *wooed of time* i.e., tempted to evil by the present times   7 *canker vice* vice like a cankerworm (which preys on buds)   9 *ambush of young days* snares of youth 10 *charged* attacked   12 *To tie up envy* to overcome malice 12 *enlarged* at liberty   13 *If some ... show* i.e., if some suspicion of evil did not surround you   14 *owe* own

71

No longer mourn for me when I am dead
Than you shall hear the surly sullen bell
Give warning to the world that I am fled
From this vile world with vilest worms to dwell.   *4*
Nay, if you read this line, remember not
The hand that writ it, for I love you so
That I in your sweet thoughts would be forgot,
If thinking on me then should make you woe.   *8*
O, if, I say, you look upon this verse,
When I, perhaps, compounded am with clay,
Do not so much as my poor name rehearse,
But let your love even with my life decay,   *12*
   Lest the wise world should look into your moan,
   And mock you with me after I am gone.

72

O, lest the world should task you to recite
What merit lived in me that you should love
After my death, dear love, forget me quite,
4   For you in me can nothing worthy prove;
Unless you would devise some virtuous lie,
To do more for me than mine own desert,
And hang more praise upon deceasèd I
8   Than niggard truth would willingly impart.
O, lest your true love may seem false in this,
That you for love speak well of me untrue,
My name be buried where my body is,
12   And live no more to shame nor me nor you;
    For I am shamed by that which I bring forth,
    And so should you, to love things nothing worth.

1 *recite* tell   4 *prove* find   6 *desert* (rhymes with "impart")
8 *niggard* miserly   10 *untrue* untruly   11 *My name be* let my
name be   12 *nor . . . nor* neither . . . nor

73

That time of year thou mayst in me behold
When yellow leaves, or none, or few, do hang
Upon those boughs which shake against the cold,
Bare ruined choirs where late the sweet birds sang.   *4*
In me thou seest the twilight of such day
As after sunset fadeth in the west,
Which by and by black night doth take away,
Death's second self, that seals up all in rest.   *8*
In me thou seest the glowing of such fire
That on the ashes of his youth doth lie,
As the deathbed whereon it must expire,
Consumed with that which it was nourished by.   *12*
   This thou perceiv'st, which makes thy love more
      strong,
   To love that well which thou must leave ere long.

---

4 *choirs* the part of the chancel in which the service is performed
7 *by and by* shortly   8 *Death's second self* i.e., sleep   8 *seals up*
encloses (with a suggestion of sealing a coffin)   10 *That* as
14 *that* i.e., that substance, the poet

74

But be contented. When that fell arrest
Without all bail shall carry me away,
My life hath in this line some interest
4 Which for memorial still with thee shall stay.
When thou reviewest this, thou dost review
The very part was consecrate to thee.
The earth can have but earth, which is his due;
8 My spirit is thine, the better part of me.
So then thou hast but lost the dregs of life,
The prey of worms, my body being dead;
The coward conquest of a wretch's knife,
12 Too base of thee to be rememberèd.
    The worth of that is that which it contains,
    And that is this, and this with thee remains.

---

1 *fell* cruel 2 *Without all bail* i.e., without any possibility of release 3 *line* verse 3 *interest* part 4 *still* always 7 *his* its 11 *The coward conquest* i.e., conquest that even a coward can make 11 *wretch's* Death's (or possibly Time's) 13–14 *The worth . . . remains* i.e., the value of the body is in the spirit it contains, and this spirit is in the poem and remains with you

75

So are you to my thoughts as food to life,
Or as sweet-seasoned showers are to the ground;
And for the peace of you I hold such strife
As 'twixt a miser and his wealth is found;   4
Now proud as an enjoyer, and anon
Doubting the filching age will steal his treasure;
Now counting best to be with you alone,
Then bettered that the world may see my pleasure;   8
Sometime all full with feasting on your sight,
And by and by clean starvèd for a look;
Possessing or pursuing no delight
Save what is had or must from you be took.   12
    Thus do I pine and surfeit day by day,
    Or gluttoning on all, or all away.

2 *sweet-seasoned* of the sweet season, spring   3 *peace of you*
i.e., the peace I find because of you   5 *enjoyer* possessor
5 *anon* soon   6 *Doubting* fearing   8 *bettered* made happier
10 *by and by* soon   10 *clean* wholly   14 *Or . . . or* either . . . or

76

Why is my verse so barren of new pride,
So far from variation or quick change?
Why with the time do I not glance aside
4   To new-found methods and to compounds strange?
Why write I still all one, ever the same,
And keep invention in a noted weed,
That every word doth almost tell my name,
8   Showing their birth, and where they did proceed?
O, know, sweet love, I always write of you,
And you and love are still my argument.
So all my best is dressing old words new,
12   Spending again what is already spent:
    For as the sun is daily new and old,
    So is my love still telling what is told.

---

1 *pride* adornment   3 *with the time* (1) following the present
fashion (2) with the passage of time   4 *compounds* (1) composi-
tions (2) compound words   5 *still all one* always one way   6 *in-
vention* imaginative creation   6 *noted weed* well-known dress
8 *where* whence   10 *argument* theme

77

Thy glass will show thee how thy beauties wear,
Thy dial how thy precious minutes waste;
The vacant leaves thy mind's imprint will bear,
And of this book this learning mayst thou taste.   *4*
The wrinkles which thy glass will truly show,
Of mouthèd graves, will give thee memory;
Thou by thy dial's shady stealth mayst know
Time's thievish progress to eternity.   *8*
Look what thy memory cannot contain,
Commit to these waste blanks, and thou shalt find
Those children nursed, delivered from thy brain,
To take a new acquaintance of thy mind.   *12*
   These offices, so oft as thou wilt look,
   Shall profit thee, and much enrich thy book.

2 *dial* sundial   3 *vacant leaves* i.e., the blank leaves (of a memorandum book, or "table" as in Sonnet 122)   6 *mouthèd* i.e., gaping, openmouthed   6 *give thee memory* remind you   7 *shady stealth* slowly moving shadow   9 *Look what* whatever   10 *waste blanks* blank pages   11 *children* i.e., your thoughts   13 *offices* duties (of looking at the mirror, the sundial, and the thoughts in the book)

78

So oft have I invoked thee for my Muse
And found such fair assistance in my verse
As every alien pen hath got my use
4 And under thee their poesy disperse.
Thine eyes, that taught the dumb on high to sing
And heavy ignorance aloft to fly,
Have added feathers to the learnèd's wing,
8 And given grace a double majesty.
Yet be most proud of that which I compile,
Whose influence is thine, and born of thee.
In others' works thou dost but mend the style,
12 And arts with thy sweet graces gracèd be;
    But thou art all my art and dost advance
    As high as learning my rude ignorance.

3 *As* that   3 *alien pen* pen belonging to others   3 *got my use*
adopted my practice (either style or subject matter)   4 *under
thee* i.e., with you as patron   5 *on high* (1) aloud (2) loftily
8 *grace* excellence   9 *compile* write   10 *influence* inspiration
14 *rude* unrefined

79

Whilst I alone did call upon thy aid,
My verse alone had all thy gentle grace;
But now my gracious numbers are decayed,
And my sick Muse doth give another place.   *4*
I grant, sweet love, thy lovely argument
Deserves the travail of a worthier pen,
Yet what of thee thy poet doth invent
He robs thee of, and pays it thee again.   *8*
He lends thee virtue, and he stole that word
From thy behavior; beauty doth he give,
And found it in thy cheek; he can afford
No praise to thee but what in thee doth live.   *12*
   Then thank him not for that which he doth say,
   Since what he owes thee thou thyself dost pay.

3 *gracious numbers* pleasing verses   4 *give another place* yield
to another   5 *thy lovely argument* the theme of your loveliness
11 *afford* offer   14 *owes* (poems are regarded as the poet's re-
payment of obligation; see Sonnet 83, line 4)

80

O, how I faint when I of you do write,
Knowing a better spirit doth use your name,
And in the praise thereof spends all his might,
4 To make me tongue-tied speaking of your fame.
But since your worth, wide as the ocean is,
The humble as the proudest sail doth bear,
My saucy bark, inferior far to his,
8 On your broad main doth willfully appear.
Your shallowest help will hold me up afloat
Whilst he upon your soundless deep doth ride;
Or, being wracked, I am a worthless boat,
12 He of tall building, and of goodly pride.
    Then if he thrive, and I be cast away,
    The worst was this: my love was my decay.

1 *faint* waver   2 *better spirit* greater genius   6 *humble* humblest
6 *as* as well as   8 *willfully* boldly   10 *soundless* bottomless
11 *wracked* wrecked   11 *boat* small vessel (in contrast to a
ship)   12 *tall building* sturdy construction   12 *pride* magnifi-
cence   14 *decay* cause of ruin

81

Or I shall live your epitaph to make,
Or you survive when I in earth am rotten.
From hence your memory death cannot take,
Although in me each part will be forgotten.   *4*
Your name from hence immortal life shall have,
Though I, once gone, to all the world must die.
The earth can yield me but a common grave,
When you entombèd in men's eyes shall lie.   *8*
Your monument shall be my gentle verse,
Which eyes not yet created shall o'erread,
And tongues to be your being shall rehearse
When all the breathers of this world are dead.   *12*
   You still shall live—such virtue hath my pen—
   Where breath most breathes, even in the mouths
      of men.

1 *Or* either   3 *From hence* from these poems (?) from the
earth (?)   4 *in me each part* all of my qualities   5 *from
hence* from these poems   11 *rehearse* repeat   13 *virtue* power
14 *breath* life

82

I grant thou wert not married to my Muse,
And therefore mayst without attaint o'erlook
The dedicated words which writers use
4   Of their fair subject, blessing every book.
Thou art as fair in knowledge as in hue,
Finding thy worth a limit past my praise;
And therefore art enforced to seek anew
8   Some fresher stamp of the time-bettering days.
And do so, love; yet when they have devised
What strainèd touches rhetoric can lend,
Thou, truly fair, wert truly sympathized
12   In true plain words by thy true-telling friend:
    And their gross painting might be better used
    Where cheeks need blood; in thee it is abused.

1 *married to* closely joined to   2 *attaint* dishonor   2 *o'erlook* read over   3 *dedicated* devoted (with a pun on dedications prefixed to books)   5 *hue* (1) complexion (2) figure   6 *limit* reach   8 *stamp* impression   8 *time-bettering* improving   11 *fair* beautiful   11 *truly sympathized* represented to the life

83

I never saw that you did painting need,
And therefore to your fair no painting set;
I found, or thought I found, you did exceed
The barren tender of a poet's debt;   4
And therefore have I slept in your report,
That you yourself, being extant, well might show
How far a modern quill doth come too short,
Speaking of worth, what worth in you doth grow.   8
This silence for my sin you did impute,
Which shall be most my glory, being dumb;
For I impair not beauty, being mute,
When others would give life and bring a tomb.   12
   There lives more life in one of your fair eyes
   Than both your poets can in praise devise.

2 *fair* beauty   4 *The barren . . . debt* i.e., the worthless offer
that the poet is obliged to make   5 *slept in your report* refrained
from praising you   7 *modern* trivial

84

Who is it that says most, which can say more
Than this rich praise, that you alone are you,
In whose confine immurèd is the store
4   Which should example where your equal grew?
Lean penury within that pen doth dwell,
That to his subject lends not some small glory,
But he that writes of you, if he can tell
8   That you are you, so dignifies his story.
Let him but copy what in you is writ,
Not making worse what nature made so clear,
And such a counterpart shall fame his wit,
12   Making his style admirèd everywhere.
     You to your beauteous blessings add a curse,
       Being fond on praise, which makes your praises
         worse.

1 *Who . . . more* i.e., who, having said the utmost, can say more
3–4 *In whose . . . grew* in whom is stored all the abundance which
would have to serve as a model for any equal   6 *his* its   10 *clear*
radiant   11 *fame his wit* make famous his mind   14 *fond on*
foolishly enamored of (but the sense seemed called for here
is that the patron's excellence is such that it wreaks havoc with
the poets who seek to praise him)

85

My tongue-tied Muse in manners holds her still
While comments of your praise, richly compiled,
Reserve their character with golden quill
And precious phrase by all the Muses filed.   4
I think good thoughts whilst other write good words,
And, like unlettered clerk, still cry "Amen"
To every hymn that able spirit affords
In polished form of well-refinèd pen.   8
Hearing you praised, I say, " 'Tis so, 'tis true,"
And to the most of praise add something more;
But that is in my thought, whose love to you,
Though words come hindmost, holds his rank   12
    before.
  Then others for the breath of words respect,
  Me for my dumb thoughts, speaking in effect.

1 *in manners holds her still* is politely silent   2–3 *While ... quill*
while comments in your praise, richly composed with golden pen,
preserve their features ("character" means both "writing" and
"traits," "features")   4 *filed* polished   5 *other* others   6 *still*
always   7 *able spirit affords* i.e., competent poets write   10 *most*
utmost   13–14 *Then others ... effect* i.e., then take notice of
other poets for their spoken words (but in "breath" there is a
suggestion of their insubstantiality), and of me for my silent
thoughts, which, by their silence, speak

86

Was it the proud full sail of his great verse,
Bound for the prize of all too precious you,
That did my ripe thoughts in my brain inhearse,
4   Making their tomb the womb wherein they grew?
Was it his spirit, by spirits taught to write
Above a mortal pitch, that struck me dead?
No, neither he, nor his compeers by night
8   Giving him aid, my verse astonishèd.
He, nor that affable familiar ghost
Which nightly gulls him with intelligence,
As victors, of my silence cannot boast;
12   I was not sick of any fear from thence.
　　But when your countenance filled up his line,
　　Then lacked I matter, that enfeebled mine.

1 *his* i.e., a rival poet's　3 *inhearse* enclose as in a coffin　6 *dead* silent　8 *astonishèd* struck dumb　9 *familiar ghost* assisting spirit　10 *gulls him with intelligence* deceives him with rumors (?)　13 *countenance filled up his line* (1) beauty was the subject of his verse (2) approval polished his verse (if the quarto's "fild" is printed "filed" instead of "filled")

87

Farewell, thou art too dear for my possessing,
And like enough thou know'st thy estimate.
The charter of thy worth gives thee releasing;
My bonds in thee are all determinate.   4
For how do I hold thee but by thy granting,
And for that riches where is my deserving?
The cause of this fair gift in me is wanting,
And so my patent back again is swerving.   8
Thyself thou gav'st, thy own worth then not
      knowing,
Or me, to whom thou gav'st it, else mistaking;
So thy great gift, upon misprision growing,
Comes home again, on better judgment making.   12
   Thus have I had thee as a dream doth flatter,
   In sleep a king, but waking no such matter.

2 *estimate* value 3 *charter* privilege 4 *bonds in* claims on
4 *determinate* expired 7 *wanting* lacking 8 *patent* privilege
8 *back again is swerving* returns (to you) 11 *upon misprision
growing* arising from a mistake

88

When thou shalt be disposed to set me light
And place my merit in the eye of scorn,
Upon thy side against myself I'll fight
4   And prove thee virtuous, though thou art forsworn.
With mine own weakness being best acquainted,
Upon thy part I can set down a story
Of faults concealed wherein I am attainted,
8   That thou in losing me shall win much glory.
And I by this will be a gainer too,
For, bending all my loving thoughts on thee,
The injuries that to myself I do,
12 Doing thee vantage, double-vantage me.
    Such is my love, to thee I so belong,
    That for thy right myself will bear all wrong.

1 *set me light* value me little   8 *That* so that   12 *vantage* advantage   14 *right* (1) good (2) privilege

89

Say that thou didst forsake me for some fault,
And I will comment upon that offense.
Speak of my lameness, and I straight will halt,
Against thy reasons making no defense.   4
Thou canst not, love, disgrace me half so ill,
To set a form upon desirèd change,
As I'll myself disgrace, knowing thy will.
I will acquaintance strangle and look strange;   8
Be absent from thy walks, and in my tongue
Thy sweet belovèd name no more shall dwell,
Lest I, too much profane, should do it wrong
And haply of our old acquaintance tell.   12
    For thee, against myself I'll vow debate,
    For I must ne'er love him whom thou dost hate.

1 *Say* i.e., assume 3 *halt* limp 4 *reasons* arguments 5 *disgrace* discredit 6 *To set . . . change* to give a good appearance to the change you desire (?) 7 *disgrace* disfigure 8 *acquaintance* i.e., familiarity 12 *haply* by chance 13 *debate* contention

90

Then hate me when thou wilt; if ever, now;
Now, while the world is bent my deeds to cross,
Join with the spite of fortune, make me bow,
4   And do not drop in for an after-loss.
Ah, do not, when my heart hath 'scaped this sorrow,
Come in the rearward of a conquered woe;
Give not a windy night a rainy morrow,
8   To linger out a purposed overthrow.
If thou wilt leave me, do not leave me last,
When other petty griefs have done their spite,
But in the onset come; so shall I taste
12 At first the very worst of fortune's might,
  And other strains of woe, which now seem woe,
  Compared with loss of thee will not seem so.

---

4 *after-loss* later loss   6 *Come in . . . woe* i.e., come belatedly
when I have conquered my sorrow   8 *linger out* prolong   8 *pur-
posed* intended   13 *strains* kinds

91

Some glory in their birth, some in their skill,
Some in their wealth, some in their body's force,
Some in their garments, though newfangled ill,
Some in their hawks and hounds, some in their
    horse;   4
And every humor hath his adjunct pleasure,
Wherein it finds a joy above the rest,
But these particulars are not my measure;
All these I better in one general best.   8
Thy love is better than high birth to me,
Richer than wealth, prouder than garments' cost,
Of more delight than hawks or horses be;
And having thee, of all men's pride I boast: 12
    Wretched in this alone, that thou mayst take
    All this away, and me most wretched make.

---

3 *newfangled ill* fashionably ugly 4 *horse* horses 5 *humor*
temperament 5 *his* its 7 *measure* standard (of happiness)
12 *all men's pride* i.e., all that men take pride in

92

But do thy worst to steal thyself away,
For term of life thou art assurèd mine,
And life no longer than thy love will stay,
4   For it depends upon that love of thine.
Then need I not to fear the worst of wrongs,
When in the least of them my life hath end.
I see a better state to me belongs
8   Than that which on thy humor doth depend.
Thou canst not vex me with inconstant mind,
Since that my life on thy revolt doth lie.
O, what a happy title do I find,
12   Happy to have thy love, happy to die!
    But what's so blessèd-fair that fears no blot?
    Thou mayst be false, and yet I know it not.

6 *the least of them* i.e., any sign that the friend's love is cooling
8 *humor* caprice   10 *Since . . . lie* since my life ends if you desert
me   11 *happy title* title to happiness

93

So shall I live, supposing thou art true,
Like a deceivèd husband; so love's face
May still seem love to me, though altered new,
Thy looks with me, thy heart in other place.   4
For there can live no hatred in thine eye;
Therefore in that I cannot know thy change.
In many's looks, the false heart's history
Is writ in moods and frowns and wrinkles strange, 8
But heaven in thy creation did decree
That in thy face sweet love should ever dwell;
Whate'er thy thoughts or thy heart's workings be,
Thy looks should nothing thence but sweetness tell. 12
   How like Eve's apple doth thy beauty grow
   If thy sweet virtue answer not thy show.

94

They that have pow'r to hurt and will do none,
That do not do the thing they most do show,
Who, moving others, are themselves as stone,
4   Unmovèd, cold, and to temptation slow;
They rightly do inherit heaven's graces
And husband nature's riches from expense;
They are the lords and owners of their faces,
8   Others but stewards of their excellence.
The summer's flow'r is to the summer sweet,
Though to itself it only live and die;
But if that flow'r with base infection meet,
12   The basest weed outbraves his dignity:
    For sweetest things turn sourest by their deeds;
    Lilies that fester smell far worse than weeds.

2 *do show* (1) seem to do (?) (2) show they could do (?)
6 *husband* manage prudently 6 *expense* loss 8 *stewards* cus-
todians 12 *outbraves his* surpasses its

95

How sweet and lovely dost thou make the shame
Which, like a canker in the fragrant rose,
Doth spot the beauty of thy budding name!
O, in what sweets dost thou thy sins enclose!   *4*
That tongue that tells the story of thy days,
Making lascivious comments on thy sport,
Cannot dispraise, but in a kind of praise;
Naming thy name blesses an ill report.   *8*
O, what a mansion have those vices got
Which for their habitation chose out thee,
Where beauty's veil doth cover every blot,
And all things turns to fair that eyes can see!   *12*
   Take heed, dear heart, of this large privilege;
   The hardest knife ill-used doth lose his edge.

2 *canker* cankerworm (that feeds on blossoms)   6 *sport* amo-
rous dalliance   14 *his* its

96

Some say thy fault is youth, some wantonness,
Some say thy grace is youth and gentle sport;
Both grace and faults are loved of more and less;
4   Thou mak'st faults graces that to thee resort.
As on the finger of a thronèd queen
The basest jewel will be well esteemed,
So are those errors that in thee are seen
8   To truths translated and for true things deemed.
How many lambs might the stern wolf betray,
If like a lamb he could his looks translate;
How many gazers might'st thou lead away,
12 If thou wouldst use the strength of all thy state!
        But do not so; I love thee in such sort
        As, thou being mine, mine is thy good report.

2 *gentle sport* amorous dalliance (a more favorable interpretation of the "wantonness" of line 1)   3 *of more and less* by people high and low   8 *translated* transformed   9 *stern* cruel   12 *state* eminent position   13–14 (this couplet ends Sonnet 36)   14 *report* reputation

97

How like a winter hath my absence been
From thee, the pleasure of the fleeting year!
What freezings have I felt, what dark days seen,
What old December's bareness everywhere!   *4*
And yet this time removed was summer's time,
The teeming autumn, big with rich increase,
Bearing the wanton burden of the prime,
Like widowed wombs after their lords' decease.   *8*
Yet this abundant issue seemed to me
But hope of orphans and unfathered fruit;
For summer and his pleasures wait on thee,
And, thou away, the very birds are mute;   *12*
    Or, if they sing, 'tis with so dull a cheer,
    That leaves look pale, dreading the winter's near.

---

2 *pleasure of the fleeting year* i.e., the summer (normally the
pleasant part of the year, but like a winter because of the friend's
absence)   6 *teeming* pregnant   7 *Bearing . . . prime* i.e., bearing
the load conceived in the wantonness of the spring (*prime* =
spring)   9 *issue* offspring   11 *his* its

98

From you have I been absent in the spring,
When proud-pied April, dressed in all his trim,
Hath put a spirit of youth in everything,
4 That heavy Saturn laughed and leaped with him,
Yet nor the lays of birds, nor the sweet smell
Of different flowers in odor and in hue,
Could make me any summer's story tell,
Or from their proud lap pluck them where they
8   grew.
Nor did I wonder at the lily's white,
Nor praise the deep vermilion in the rose;
They were but sweet, but figures of delight,
12 Drawn after you, you pattern of all those.
    Yet seemed it winter still, and, you away,
    As with your shadow I with these did play.

2 *proud-pied* gorgeously variegated   2 *trim* ornamental dress
4 *That* so that   4 *heavy Saturn* (the planet Saturn was thought
to cause gloominess)   5 *nor . . . nor* neither . . . nor   5 *lays*
songs   7 *summer's story* i.e., pleasant stories suitable for sum-
mer ("a sad tale's best for winter")   14 *shadow* portrait

99

The forward violet thus did I chide:
Sweet thief, whence didst thou steal thy sweet that
    smells
If not from my love's breath? The purple pride
Which on thy soft cheek for complexion dwells   *4*
In my love's veins thou hast too grossly dyed.
The lily I condemnèd for thy hand,
And buds of marjoram had stol'n thy hair;
The roses fearfully on thorns did stand,   *8*
One blushing shame, another white despair;
A third, nor red nor white, had stol'n of both,
And to his robb'ry had annexed thy breath;
But for his theft, in pride of all his growth   *12*
A vengeful canker eat him up to death.
    More flowers I noted, yet I none could see,
    But sweet or color it had stol'n from thee.

---

1 *forward* early   3 *purple* (Shakespeare often does not distin-
guish between purple and crimson)   3 *pride* splendor   6 *con-
demnèd for thy hand* condemned for stealing the whiteness of
your hand   8 *fearfully* uneasily   13 *canker eat* cankerworm ate

100

Where art thou, Muse, that thou forget'st so long
To speak of that which gives thee all thy might?
Spend'st thou thy fury on some worthless song,
4 Dark'ning thy pow'r to lend base subjects light?
Return, forgetful Muse, and straight redeem
In gentle numbers time so idly spent,
Sing to the ear that doth thy lays esteem,
8 And gives thy pen both skill and argument.
Rise, resty Muse, my love's sweet face survey,
If Time have any wrinkle graven there;
If any, be a satire to decay
12 And make Time's spoils despisèd everywhere.
    Give my love fame faster than Time wastes life;
    So thou prevent'st his scythe and crooked knife.

3 *fury* poetic enthusiasm   6 *numbers* verses   7 *lays* songs   8 *argument* subject   9 *resty* torpid   10 *If* to see if   11 *be a satire to decay* satirize decay

101

O truant Muse, what shall be thy amends
For thy neglect of truth in beauty dyed?
Both truth and beauty on my love depends;
So dost thou too, and therein dignified.   *4*
Make answer, Muse, wilt thou not haply say,
"Truth needs no color, with his color fixed,
Beauty no pencil, beauty's truth to lay;
But best is best, if never intermixed?"   *8*
Because he needs no praise, wilt thou be dumb?
Excuse not silence so, for't lies in thee
To make him much outlive a gilded tomb,
And to be praised of ages yet to be.   *12*
    Then do thy office, Muse; I teach thee how
    To make him seem, long hence, as he shows now.

3 *love* beloved   4 *dignified* you are dignified   5 *haply* perchance
6 *color* artificial color, disguise   6 *his color fixed* its unchange-
able color   7 *to lay* i.e., to put on canvas   8 *intermixed* i.e., with
the inadequate words of the Muse   13 *do thy office* perform your
duty

102

My love is strength'ned, though more weak in
    seeming;
I love not less, though less the show appear.
That love is merchandized whose rich esteeming
4 The owner's tongue doth publish everywhere.
Our love was new, and then but in the spring,
When I was wont to greet it with my lays,
As Philomel in summer's front doth sing
8 And stops her pipe in growth of riper days.
Not that the summer is less pleasant now
Than when her mournful hymns did hush the night,
But that wild music burdens every bough,
12 And sweets grown common lose their dear delight.
    Therefore, like her, I sometime hold my tongue,
    Because I would not dull you with my song.

2 *show* outward manifestation   3 *merchandized* offered for sale,
hawked   3 *esteeming* value   6 *lays* songs   7 *Philomel* the night-
ingale   7 *front* forefront   8 *riper* later   11 *But that* i.e., but it
seems so because

103

Alack, what poverty my Muse brings forth,
That, having such a scope to show her pride,
The argument all bare is of more worth
Than when it hath my added praise beside.   *4*
O, blame me not if I no more can write!
Look in your glass, and there appears a face
That overgoes my blunt invention quite,
Dulling my lines and doing me disgrace.   *8*
Were it not sinful then, striving to mend,
To mar the subject that before was well?
For to no other pass my verses tend
Than of your graces and your gifts to tell;   *12*
　　And more, much more, than in my verse can sit
　　Your own glass shows you when you look in it.

1 *poverty* inferior matter   2 *pride* splendor   3 *argument* theme
3 *all bare* i.e., of itself   7 *overgoes my blunt invention* exceeds
my awkward creation   8 *disgrace* discredit   9 *mend* improve
11 *pass* purpose

104

To me, fair friend, you never can be old,
For as you were when first your eye I eyed,
Such seems your beauty still. Three winters cold
4   Have from the forests shook three summers' pride,
Three beauteous springs to yellow autumn turned
In process of the seasons have I seen,
Three April perfumes in three hot Junes burned,
8   Since first I saw you fresh, which yet are green.
Ah, yet doth beauty, like a dial hand,
Steal from his figure, and no pace perceived;
So your sweet hue, which methinks still doth stand,
12   Hath motion, and mine eye may be deceived;
     For fear of which, hear this, thou age unbred:
     Ere you were born was beauty's summer dead.

4 *pride* splendor   10 *his figure* its numeral (with a pun on "figure," the friend's appearance)   11 *sweet hue* fair appearance
11 *still* (1) motionless (2) always, forever   13 *unbred* unborn

105

Let not my love be called idolatry,
Nor my belovèd as an idol show,
Since all alike my songs and praises be
To one, of one, still such, and ever so.   *4*
Kind is my love today, tomorrow kind,
Still constant in a wondrous excellence;
Therefore my verse, to constancy confined,
One thing expressing, leaves out difference.   *8*
Fair, kind, and true is all my argument,
Fair, kind, and true, varying to other words;
And in this change is my invention spent,
Three themes in one, which wondrous scope affords.   *12*
    Fair, kind, and true have often lived alone,
    Which three till now never kept seat in one.

4 *still* always   5 *Kind* naturally benevolent   8 *difference* variety
9 *Fair* beautiful   9 *argument* theme   11 *And in . . . spent* i.e.,
and in variations on this theme I expend all my imagination

106

When in the chronicle of wasted time
I see descriptions of the fairest wights,
And beauty making beautiful old rhyme
4   In praise of ladies dead and lovely knights;
Then, in the blazon of sweet beauty's best,
Of hand, of foot, of lip, of eye, of brow,
I see their antique pen would have expressed
8   Even such a beauty as you master now.
So all their praises are but prophecies
Of this our time, all you prefiguring,
And, for they looked but with divining eyes,
12   They had not still enough your worth to sing:
       For we, which now behold these present days,
       Have eyes to wonder, but lack tongues to praise.

1 *wasted* past   2 *wights* people   4 *lovely* attractive   5 *blazon* commemorative description   11 *for* because   11 *divining* guessing   12 *still* yet (the common emendation to "skill" is unnecessary)   13 *For* for even

107

Not mine own fears nor the prophetic soul
Of the wide world dreaming on things to come
Can yet the lease of my true love control,
Supposed as forfeit to a confined doom.   *4*
The mortal moon hath her eclipse endured,
And the sad augurs mock their own presage,
Incertainties now crown themselves assured,
And peace proclaims olives of endless age.   *8*
Now with the drops of this most balmy time
My love looks fresh, and Death to me subscribes,
Since, spite of him, I'll live in this poor rhyme,
While he insults o'er dull and speechless tribes: *12*
    And thou in this shalt find thy monument,
    When tyrants' crests and tombs of brass are spent.

3 *lease* allotted time   4 *Supposed . . . doom* i.e., though it is
thought doomed to expire after a limited time   5 *The mortal
moon . . . endured* (numerous commentators claim that this line
dates the sonnet; among interpretations are: 1588, when the
Spanish Armada, thought to have assumed a crescent formation,
was destroyed; 1595, when the moon underwent a total eclipse;
1595, when Queen Elizabeth I survived a critical period in her
horoscope; 1599, when Queen Elizabeth survived an illness)
6–7 *And the sad . . . assured* and the prophets of gloom are
mocked by their own predictions now that uncertainties yield to
assurance (?)   10 *to me subscribes* acknowledges me as his su-
perior   12 *insults* triumphs   14 *spent* consumed

108

What's in the brain that ink may character
Which hath not figured to thee my true spirit?
What's new to speak, what now to register,
4   That may express my love or thy dear merit?
Nothing, sweet boy, but yet, like prayers divine,
I must each day say o'er the very same;
Counting no old thing old, thou mine, I thine,
8   Even as when first I hallowed thy fair name.
So that eternal love in love's fresh case
Weighs not the dust and injury of age,
Nor gives to necessary wrinkles place,
12   But makes antiquity for aye his page,
        Finding the first conceit of love there bred
        Where time and outward form would show it
            dead.

1 *character* write   2 *figured* shown   9 *fresh case* youthful appearance   10 *Weighs not* cares not for   12 *for aye his page* forever his servant   13 *conceit* conception

109

O, never say that I was false of heart,
Though absence seemed my flame to qualify.
As easy might I from myself depart
As from my soul, which in thy breast doth lie.   *4*
That is my home of love; if I have ranged,
Like him that travels, I return again,
Just to the time, not with the time exchanged,
So that myself bring water for my stain.   *8*
Never believe, though in my nature reigned
All frailties that besiege all kinds of blood,
That it could so preposterously be stained
To leave for nothing all thy sum of good;   *12*
   For nothing this wide universe I call
   Save thou, my Rose; in it thou art my all.

---

2 *qualify* moderate   5 *ranged* wandered   7 *Just* punctual   7 *exchanged* changed   10 *blood* flesh, temperament

110

Alas, 'tis true I have gone here and there
And made myself a motley to the view,
Gored mine own thoughts, sold cheap what is most
    dear,
4 Made old offenses of affections new.
Most true it is that I have looked on truth
Askance and strangely; but, by all above,
These blenches gave my heart another youth,
8 And worse essays proved thee my best of love.
Now all is done, have what shall have no end.
Mine appetite I never more will grind
On newer proof, to try an older friend,
12 A god in love, to whom I am confined.
    Then give me welcome, next my heaven the best,
    Even to thy pure and most most loving breast.

2 *motley* jester 3 *Gored* wounded 4 *affections* passions 5 *truth* fidelity 6 *strangely* in a reserved manner 7 *blenches* side glances (?) 8 *worse essays* trials of worse friendships (?) 9 *have what shall have no end* take what shall be eternal 11 *proof* experiment 11 *try* test 13 *next* next to

111

O, for my sake do you with Fortune chide,
The guilty goddess of my harmful deeds,
That did not better for my life provide
Than public means which public manners breeds.   *4*
Thence comes it that my name receives a brand,
And almost thence my nature is subdued
To what it works in, like the dyer's hand.
Pity me then, and wish I were renewed,   *8*
Whilst, like a willing patient, I will drink
Potions of eisel 'gainst my strong infection;
No bitterness that I will bitter think,
Nor double penance, to correct correction.   *12*
    Pity me then, dear friend, and I assure ye
    Even that your pity is enough to cure me.

---

3 *That* who   3 *life* livelihood   4 *Than . . . breeds* than earning a
livelihood by satisfying the public, which engenders vulgar man-
ners   5 *brand* stigma   6–7 *subdued/To* subjected to   10 *eisel*
vinegar (used as a preventative against the plague)

112

Your love and pity doth th' impression fill,
Which vulgar scandal stamped upon my brow;
For what care I who calls me well or ill,
4   So you o'er-green my bad, my good allow?
You are my all the world, and I must strive
To know my shames and praises from your tongue;
None else to me, nor I to none alive,
8   That my steeled sense or changes right or wrong.
In so profound abysm I throw all care
Of others' voices, that my adder's sense
To critic and to flatterer stoppèd are.
12   Mark how with my neglect I do dispense:
          You are so strongly in my purpose bred,
          That all the world besides methinks are dead.

1 *doth th' impression fill* effaces the scar   2 *stamped* (allusion to branding felons)   4 *allow* approve   6 *shames* faults   7–8 *None else . . . wrong* only you can change my sense of what is right and wrong (?)   9 *profound* deep   10 *adder's sense* i.e., deaf ears (adders were thought to be deaf)   12 *Mark how . . . dispense* listen to how I excuse ("dispense with") my neglect (i.e., of others)   13 *in my purpose bred* grown in my mind   14 *That all . . . dead* that I think only you have life

113

Since I left you, mine eye is in my mind,
And that which governs me to go about
Doth part his function and is partly blind,
Seems seeing, but effectually is out;   *4*
For it no form delivers to the heart
Of bird, of flow'r, or shape, which it doth latch.
Of his quick objects hath the mind no part,
Nor his own vision holds what it doth catch;   *8*
For if it see the rud'st or gentlest sight,
The most sweet favor or deformèd'st creature,
The mountain, or the sea, the day, or night,
The crow, or dove, it shapes them to your feature.   *12*
    Incapable of more, replete with you,
    My most true mind thus maketh mine eye untrue.

3 *Doth part . . . blind* i.e., performs only part of its function, receiving images but not conveying them to the mind or "heart" 3, 7, 8 *his* its   4 *effectually* in reality   6 *latch* catch sight of 7 *quick* fleeting   10 *favor* face   13 *Incapable of* unable to take in   14 *true* faithful

114

Or whether doth my mind, being crowned with you,
Drink up the monarch's plague, this flattery?
Or whether shall I say mine eye saith true,
4   And that your love taught it this alchemy,
To make of monsters, and things indigest,
Such cherubins as your sweet self resemble,
Creating every bad a perfect best
8   As fast as objects to his beams assemble?
O, 'tis the first, 'tis flatt'ry in my seeing,
And my great mind most kingly drinks it up.
Mine eye well knows what with his gust is 'greeing,
12 And to his palate doth prepare the cup.
    If it be poisoned, 'tis the lesser sin
    That mine eye loves it and doth first begin.

1, 3 *Or whether* (indicates alternative questions)   **1** *being crowned with you* made a king by possessing you   **2** *this flattery* i.e., false appearances (such as surround a monarch) as specified in the previous sonnet   **5** *indigest* formless   **6** *cherubins* angelic creatures   **8** *to his beams assemble* appear to his eye (the eye was thought to cast beams; see Sonnet 20, line 6)   **11** *with his gust is 'greeing* agrees with the mind's taste   **14** *That* since

115

Those lines that I before have writ do lie,
Even those that said I could not love you dearer.
Yet then my judgment knew no reason why
My most full flame should afterwards burn clearer. 4
But reckoning Time, whose millioned accidents
Creep in 'twixt vows and change decrees of kings,
Tan sacred beauty, blunt the sharp'st intents,
Divert strong minds to th' course of alt'ring things. 8
Alas, why, fearing of Time's tyranny,
Might I not then say, "Now I love you best,"
When I was certain o'er incertainty,
Crowning the present, doubting of the rest? 12
    Love is a babe; then might I not say so,
      To give full growth to that which still doth grow.

---

5 *millioned accidents* innumerable happenings 7 *Tan* i.e.,
darken, coarsen 8 *Divert* alter 12 *Crowning* glorifying 13
then therefore 13 *so* i.e., "Now I love you best" (line 10)

116

Let me not to the marriage of true minds
Admit impediments; love is not love
Which alters when it alteration finds,
4 Or bends with the remover to remove.
O, no, it is an ever-fixèd mark
That looks on tempests and is never shaken;
It is the star to every wand'ring bark,
Whose worth's unknown, although his height be
8   taken.
Love's not Time's fool, though rosy lips and cheeks
Within his bending sickle's compass come;
Love alters not with his brief hours and weeks,
12 But bears it out even to the edge of doom.
   If this be error and upon me proved,
   I never writ, nor no man ever loved.

2 *impediments* (an echo of the marriage service in the Book of
Common Prayer: "If any of you know cause or just impediment
. . .")   5 *mark* seamark   7 *the star* the North Star   8 *Whose
worth's . . . taken* whose value (e.g., to mariners) is inestimable
although the star's altitude has been determined   9 *fool* play-
thing   10 *compass* range, circle   11 *his* Time's   12 *bears it out*
survives   12 *edge of doom* Judgment Day   13 *upon* against

117

Accuse me thus: that I have scanted all
Wherein I should your great deserts repay,
Forgot upon your dearest love to call,
Whereto all bonds do tie me day by day;   *4*
That I have frequent been with unknown minds,
And given to time your own dear-purchased right;
That I have hoisted sail to all the winds
Which should transport me farthest from your sight.   *8*
Book both my willfulness and errors down,
And on just proof surmise accumulate;
Bring me within the level of your frown,
But shoot not at me in your wakened hate;   *12*
    Since my appeal says I did strive to prove
    The constancy and virtue of your love.

---

1 *scanted all* given only grudgingly   5 *frequent* intimate   5 *un-
known minds* i.e., nonentities   6 *given to time* squandered on
other people of the time   9 *Book* write down in a book   10 *sur-
mise accumulate* add suspicions   11 *level* range, aim   13 *appeal*
plea   13 *prove* test

118

Like as to make our appetites more keen
With eager compounds we our palate urge,
As to prevent our maladies unseen,
4   We sicken to shun sickness when we purge;
Even so, being full of your ne'er-cloying sweetness,
To bitter sauces did I frame my feeding;
And, sick of welfare, found a kind of meetness
8   To be diseased ere that there was true needing.
Thus policy in love, t' anticipate
The ills that were not, grew to faults assured,
And brought to medicine a healthful state,
12   Which, rank of goodness, would by ill be cured.
   But thence I learn, and find the lesson true,
   Drugs poison him that so fell sick of you.

2 *eager compounds* tart sauces 2 *urge* stimulate 3 *prevent*
forestall 6 *bitter sauces* i.e., undesirable people 6 *frame* direct
7 *sick of welfare* gorged with well-being 7 *meetness* fitness
9 *policy* prudence 11 *medicine* i.e., the need of medicine
12 *rank of* gorged with

119

What potions have I drunk of Siren tears
Distilled from limbecks foul as hell within,
Applying fears to hopes and hopes to fears,
Still losing when I saw myself to win!   *4*
What wretched errors hath my heart committed,
Whilst it hath thought itself so blessèd never!
How have mine eyes out of their spheres been fitted
In the distraction of this madding fever!   *8*
O, benefit of ill: now I find true
That better is by evil still made better;
And ruined love, when it is built anew,
Grows fairer than at first, more strong, far greater.   *12*
   So I return rebuked to my content,
   And gain by ills thrice more than I have spent.

2 *limbecks* alembics   3 *Applying* i.e., as an ointment   4 *Still*
always   6 *so blessèd never* never so blessed   7 *spheres* sockets
7 *fitted* forced by fits

120

That you were once unkind befriends me now,
And for that sorrow which I then did feel
Needs must I under my transgression bow,
4 Unless my nerves were brass or hammered steel.
For if you were by my unkindness shaken,
As I by yours, y'have passed a hell of time,
And I, a tyrant, have no leisure taken
8 To weigh how once I suffered in your crime.
O, that our night of woe might have rememb'red
My deepest sense how hard true sorrow hits,
And soon to you, as you to me then, tend'red
12 The humble salve which wounded bosoms fits!
  But that your trespass now becomes a fee;
  Mine ransoms yours, and yours must ransom me.

2 *for* because of   4 *nerves* sinews   7–8 *no leisure . . . weigh* not
taken the time to consider   9 *night of woe* i.e., estrangement
9 *rememb'red* reminded   11 *soon* as soon   11 *tend'red* offered
12 *humble salve* balm of humility   12 *fits* suits   13 *that your
trespass* that trespass of yours   13 *fee* compensation   14 *ran-
soms* atones for

121

'Tis better to be vile than vile esteemed
When not to be receives reproach of being,
And the just pleasure lost, which is so deemed
Not by our feeling, but by others' seeing.   *4*
For why should others' false adulterate eyes
Give salutation to my sportive blood?
Or on my frailties why are frailer spies,
Which in their wills count bad what I think good?   *8*
No, I am that I am, and they that level
At my abuses reckon up their own;
I may be straight though they themselves be bevel.
By their rank thoughts my deeds must not be shown,   *12*
   Unless this general evil they maintain:
   All men are bad and in their badness reign.

---

2 *being* i.e., being vile   3 *just* legitimate   3 *so* i.e., vile   6 *Give salutation to* act on   6 *sportive* wanton   8 *in their wills* i.e., willfully (?)   9 *that* who (an echo of Exodus 3:14)   9 *level* aim   10 *abuses* transgressions   11 *bevel* i.e., crooked   12 *rank* corrupt

122

Thy gift, thy tables, are within my brain
Full charactered with lasting memory,
Which shall above that idle rank remain
4 Beyond all date, even to eternity;
Or, at the least, so long as brain and heart
Have faculty by nature to subsist,
Till each to rased oblivion yield his part
8 Of thee, thy record never can be missed.
That poor retention could not so much hold,
Nor need I tallies thy dear love to score.
Therefore to give them from me was I bold,
12 To trust those tables that receive thee more.
　　To keep an adjunct to remember thee
　　Were to import forgetfulness in me.

1 *tables* memorandum books   2 *charactered* written   3 *that idle rank* that useless series of leaves   7 *rased oblivion* oblivion which erases   7 *his* its   9 *That poor retention* i.e., the memorandum books   10 *tallies* accounting devices   12 *those tables* i.e., the mind   14 *import* imply

123

No, Time, thou shalt not boast that I do change.
Thy pyramids built up with newer might
To me are nothing novel, nothing strange;
They are but dressings of a former sight.   *4*
Our dates are brief, and therefore we admire
What thou dost foist upon us that is old,
And rather make them born to our desire
Than think that we before have heard them told.   *8*
Thy registers and thee I both defy,
Not wond'ring at the present, nor the past;
For thy records and what we see doth lie,
Made more or less by thy continual haste.   *12*
　　This I do vow, and this shall ever be:
　　I will be true despite thy scythe and thee.

---

2 *pyramids* (possibly an allusion to Egyptian obelisks erected in
Rome by Pope Sextus 1586–89; more likely an allusion to tri-
umphal structures erected in London to welcome James I in
1603; most likely a reference to all monuments)　**5** *dates* allotted
times　**5** *admire* regard with wonder　**7** *born to our desire* turn
them into the new things we wish to see　**9** *registers* records

124

If my dear love were but the child of state,
It might for Fortune's bastard be unfathered,
As subject to Time's love, or to Time's hate,
Weeds among weeds, or flowers with flowers
4   gathered.
No, it was builded far from accident;
It suffers not in smiling pomp, nor falls
Under the blow of thrallèd discontent,
8   Whereto th' inviting time our fashion calls.
It fears not Policy, that heretic,
Which works on leases of short-numb'red hours,
But all alone stands hugely politic,
That it nor grows with heat, nor drowns with
12   showers.
     To this I witness call the fools of Time,
     Which die for goodness, who have lived for crime.

1 *love* i.e., the emotion, not the person   1 *but* only   1 *child of state* i.e., product of externals such as wealth and power   2 *for Fortune's bastard be unfathered* i.e., be marked as the bastard son of Fortune   5 *accident* chance   7 *thrallèd discontent* discontent of persons oppressed   9 *Policy, that heretic* i.e., unprincipled self-interest which is faithless   11 *all alone stands hugely politic* i.e., only love is infinitely prudent   12 *That it nor . . . nor* since it neither . . . nor   13 *fools of Time* playthings of Time (?) time-servers (?)   14 *Which . . . crime* i.e., who at the last minute repent their criminal lives

125

Were't aught to me I bore the canopy,
With my extern the outward honoring,
Or laid great bases for eternity,
Which proves more short than waste or ruining?   *4*
Have I not seen dwellers on form and favor
Lose all and more by paying too much rent,
For compound sweet forgoing simple savor,
Pitiful thrivers, in their gazing spent?   *8*
No, let me be obsequious in thy heart,
And take thou my oblation, poor but free,
Which is not mixed with seconds, knows no art,
But mutual render, only me for thee.   *12*
   Hence, thou suborned informer! A true soul
   When most impeached stands least in thy control.

1 *Were't aught* would it be anything   1 *canopy* (borne over an
eminent person)   2 *extern* outward action   5 *dwellers on form
and favor* i.e., those who make much of appearance and external
beauty   6 *paying too much rent* i.e., obsequiousness   7 *simple*
pure   8 *Pitiful . . . spent* pitiable creatures who use themselves
up in looking at outward honor   9 *obsequious* devoted   11 *sec-
onds* i.e., baser matter   11 *art* artifice   12 *render* surrender
13 *suborned informer* perjured witness   14 *impeached* accused

126

O thou, my lovely boy, who in thy power
Dost hold Time's fickle glass, his sickle hour,
Who hast by waning grown, and therein show'st
4   Thy lovers withering, as thy sweet self grow'st;
If Nature, sovereign mistress over wrack,
As thou goest onwards, still will pluck thee back,
She keeps thee to this purpose, that her skill
8   May Time disgrace and wretched minutes kill.
Yet fear her, O thou minion of her pleasure;
She may detain, but not still keep her treasure.
     Her audit, though delayed, answered must be,
12   And her quietus is to render thee.

2 *glass* mirror   2 *hour* hourglass   3 *by waning grown* i.e., by
growing older growing more beautiful   5 *wrack* destruction
6, 10 *still* always   9 *minion* favorite   11 *audit* final account
11 *answered* paid   12 *quietus* final settlement   12 *render* sur-
render

127

In the old age black was not counted fair,
Or, if it were, it bore not beauty's name.
But now is black beauty's successive heir,
And beauty slandered with a bastard shame; 4
For since each hand hath put on nature's power,
Fairing the foul with art's false borrowed face,
Sweet beauty hath no name, no holy bower,
But is profaned, if not lives in disgrace. 8
Therefore my mistress' eyes are raven black,
Her eyes so suited, and they mourners seem,
At such who, not born fair, no beauty lack,
Sland'ring creation with a false esteem: 12
    Yet so they mourn, becoming of their woe,
    That every tongue says beauty should look so.

1 *old age* i.e., age of chivalry 1 *black* i.e., brunette 1 *fair* beautiful (with a pun on the obvious meaning) 3 *successive heir* legitimate heir 4 *And beauty . . . shame* i.e., blond beauty is defamed as illegitimate 5 *put on* taken over 6 *art's false borrowed face* i.e., cosmetics 7 *Sweet* natural, i.e., blond 11 *At* for 13 *becoming of* gracing

128

How oft, when thou, my music, music play'st
Upon that blessèd wood whose motion sounds
With thy sweet fingers when thou gently sway'st
The wiry concord that mine ear confounds,
Do I envy those jacks that nimble leap
To kiss the tender inward of thy hand,
Whilst my poor lips, which should that harvest reap,
At the wood's boldness by thee blushing stand.
To be so tickled, they would change their state
And situation with those dancing chips
O'er whom thy fingers walk with gentle gait,
Making dead wood more blest than living lips.
  Since saucy jacks so happy are in this,
  Give them thy fingers, me thy lips to kiss.

2 *wood* keys (of the spinet or virginal)   2 *motion* movement
3 *thou gently sway'st* you gently direct   4 *wiry concord* har-
mony of the strings   4 *confounds* delightfully overcomes   5 *jacks*
(devices which pluck the strings, but here probably misused for
keys; in line 13, there is a pun on the meaning "fellows")
9 *they* i.e., the poet's lips

5–6 There are always some who cannot bear to think that
the Swan of Avon could ever make a mistake about anything.
A certain E. W. Naylor explains these lines as follows. "The
lady, having removed the rail which ordinarily stops the 'jacks'
from jumping right out of the instrument when the keys are
struck, was leaning over her work, testing it by striking the
defective note, and holding the 'tender inward' of her hand over
the 'jack' to prevent it from flying to the other end of the room."
                                                    W.H.A.

129

Th' expense of spirit in a waste of shame
Is lust in action; and, till action, lust
Is perjured, murd'rous, bloody, full of blame,
Savage, extreme, rude, cruel, not to trust;   *4*
Enjoyed no sooner but despisèd straight;
Past reason hunted, and no sooner had,
Past reason hated as a swallowed bait
On purpose laid to make the taker mad;   *8*
Made in pursuit, and in possession so;
Had, having, and in quest to have, extreme;
A bliss in proof, and proved, a very woe,
Before, a joy proposed; behind, a dream.   *12*
    All this the world well knows, yet none knows
        well
    To shun the heaven that leads men to this hell.

(handwritten: Key variant lines: 4 9 10)

1 *expense* expenditure   1 *spirit* vital power, semen   6, 7 *Past*
beyond   9 *Made* i.e., made mad (most editors emend to "Mad")
11 *in proof* while being experienced   11 *proved* i.e., when ex-
perienced   12 *dream* nightmare (?)   14 *heaven* the sensation
(or place?) of bliss

130

My mistress' eyes are nothing like the sun;
Coral is far more red than her lips' red;
If snow be white, why then her breasts are dun;
4 If hairs be wires, black wires grow on her head.
I have seen roses damasked, red and white,
But no such roses see I in her cheeks,
And in some perfumes is there more delight
8 Than in the breath that from my mistress reeks.
I love to hear her speak, yet well I know
That music hath a far more pleasing sound.
I grant I never saw a goddess go;
12 My mistress when she walks treads on the ground.
    And yet, by heaven, I think my love as rare
    As any she belied with false compare.

5 *damasked* mingled red and white 8 *reeks* emanates 11 *go* walk 14 *she* woman 14 *compare* comparison

131

Thou art as tyrannous, so as thou art,
As those whose beauties proudly make them cruel;
For well thou know'st to my dear doting heart
Thou art the fairest and most precious jewel.   *4*
Yet, in good faith, some say that thee behold,
Thy face hath not the power to make love groan;
To say they err I dare not be so bold,
Although I swear it to myself alone.   *8*
And, to be sure that is not false I swear,
A thousand groans, but thinking on thy face,
One on another's neck, do witness bear
Thy black is fairest in my judgment's place.   *12*
    In nothing art thou black save in thy deeds,
    And thence this slander, as I think, proceeds.

---

1 *so as thou art* i.e., even though you are black and not beautiful
3 *dear* loving   10 *but thinking on* when I but think of   11 *One on another's neck* i.e., in quick succession   12 *in my judgment's place* in the place assigned it by my judgment   13 *black* foul

132

Thine eyes I love, and they, as pitying me,
Knowing thy heart torment me with disdain,
Have put on black and loving mourners be,
4 Looking with pretty ruth upon my pain.
And truly not the morning sun of heaven
Better becomes the gray cheeks of the east,
Nor that full star that ushers in the even
8 Doth half that glory to the sober west
As those two mourning eyes become thy face.
O, let it then as well beseem thy heart
To mourn for me, since mourning doth thee grace,
12 And suit thy pity like in every part.
      Then will I swear beauty herself is black,
      And all they foul that thy complexion lack.

2 *torment* to torment   4 *ruth* pity   7 *even* evening   9 *mourning* (with a pun on "morning")   12 *suit thy pity like* clothe thy pity alike   14 *foul* ugly

133

Beshrew that heart that makes my heart to groan
For that deep wound it gives my friend and me.
Is't not enough to torture me alone,
But slave to slavery my sweet'st friend must be?   4
Me from myself thy cruel eye hath taken,
And my next self thou harder hast engrossed.
Of him, myself, and thee, I am forsaken;
A torment thrice threefold thus to be crossed.   8
Prison my heart in thy steel bosom's ward,
But then my friend's heart let my poor heart bail;
Whoe'er keeps me, let my heart be his guard;
Thou canst not then use rigor in my jail.   12
    And yet thou wilt, for I, being pent in thee,
    Perforce am thine, and all that is in me.

---

1 *Beshrew* curse (mild imprecation)   2 *For* because of   6 *my next self* i.e., my friend   6 *engrossed* captured   8 *crossed* thwarted   9 *ward* cell   10 *bail* go bail for, i.e., free   11 *keeps* guards   11 *guard* guardhouse   12 *rigor* cruelty   12 *my jail* i.e., my heart

134

So, now I have confessed that he is thine
And I myself am mortgaged to thy will,
Myself I'll forfeit, so that other mine
4   Thou wilt restore to be my comfort still.
But thou wilt not, nor he will not be free,
For thou art covetous, and he is kind;
He learned but surety-like to write for me
8   Under that bond that him as fast doth bind.
The statute of thy beauty thou wilt take,
Thou usurer that put'st forth all to use,
And sue a friend came debtor for my sake;
12 So him I lose through my unkind abuse.
    Him have I lost, thou hast both him and me;
    He pays the whole, and yet am I not free.

2 *will* (1) purpose (2) carnal desire (perhaps with puns on
Shakespeare's name and the name of the friend)   3 *so* provided
that   3 *other mine* i.e., my friend   4 *still* always   7–8 *He
learned . . . bind* (perhaps the idea is that the friend, as proxy,
wooed the woman for the poet but is now in her bondage)
9 *statute* security   10 *use* usury   11 *came* who became (?)
12 *my unkind abuse* unkind deception of me

135

Whoever hath her wish, thou hast thy *Will*,
And *Will* to boot, and *Will* in overplus;
More than enough am I that vex thee still,
To thy sweet will making addition thus.   *4*
Wilt thou, whose will is large and spacious,
Not once vouchsafe to hide my will in thine?
Shall will in others seem right gracious,
And in my will no fair acceptance shine?   *8*
The sea, all water, yet receives rain still
And in abundance addeth to his store;
So thou being rich in *Will* add to thy *Will*
One will of mine, to make thy large *Will* more.   *12*
   Let no unkind, no fair beseechers kill;
   Think all but one, and me in that one *Will*.

1 *Will* (1) a person named Will (perhaps the poet, perhaps the
friend, perhaps the woman's husband, perhaps all; *Will* is capital-
ized and italicized in this and in the next sonnet wherever it so
appears in the quarto) (2) desire, volition   3, 9 *still* always
4 *making addition thus* i.e., by adding myself   5, 7 (rhyming
words are trisyllabic)   6 *vouchsafe* consent   10 *his* its   13 *no
unkind* no unkind act, word, or person   13 *no fair beseechers*
i.e., any applicants for your favors (?)   14 *Think all . . . Will*
think all Wills as one and include me in that one
13 So in Q and a perfectly possible reading. Personally, how-
ever, I am inclined to accept Malone's emendation, *Let no un-
kind No fair beseechers kill*, which makes *No* a noun and *fair
beseechers* the object of the verb *kill*.   W.H.A.

136

If thy soul check thee that I come so near,
Swear to thy blind soul that I was thy *Will*,
And will, thy soul knows, is admitted there;
4   Thus far for love my love-suit, sweet, fulfill.
Will will fulfill the treasure of thy love,
Ay, fill it full with wills, and my will one.
In things of great receipt with ease we prove
8   Among a number one is reckoned none.
Then in the number let me pass untold,
Though in thy store's account I one must be;
For nothing hold me, so it please thee hold
12   That nothing me, a something, sweet, to thee.
       Make but my name thy love, and love that still,
       And then thou lovest me for my name is *Will*.

1 *check* rebuke   1 *come so near* (1) touch to the quick (2)
come so near to your bed   5 *fulfill the treasure* fill the treasury
6 *one* one of them   7 *things of great receipt* i.e., large matters
8 *Among . . . none* ("one is no number" was an Elizabethan
saying)   9 *untold* uncounted   10 *thy store's account* i.e., the in-
ventory of your supply (of lovers)   13 *my name* i.e., will, carnal
desire (?)   13 *still* always

137

Thou blind fool, Love, what dost thou to mine eyes
That they behold and see not what they see?
They know what beauty is, see where it lies,
Yet what the best is take the worst to be.   *4*
If eyes, corrupt by overpartial looks,
Be anchored in the bay where all men ride,
Why of eyes' falsehood has thou forgèd hooks,
Whereto the judgment of my heart is tied?   *8*
Why should my heart think that a several plot,
Which my heart knows the wide world's common
     place?
Or mine eyes seeing this, say this is not,
To put fair truth upon so foul a face?   *12*
   In things right true my heart and eyes have erred,
   And to this false plague are they now transferred.

3 *lies* inhabits   5 *corrupt* corrupted   6 *ride* (pun on the sense
"to mount sexually")   9 *that a several plot* that place a private
field   10 *common place* open field (with a pun on *common* =
promiscuous)   12 *To* so as to   14 *plague* (1) plague of false-
ness (2) mistress

138

When my love swears that she is made of truth,
I do believe her though I know she lies,
That she might think me some untutored youth,
4   Unlearnèd in the world's false subtleties.
Thus vainly thinking that she thinks me young,
Although she knows my days are past the best,
Simply I credit her false-speaking tongue;
8   On both sides thus is simple truth suppressed.
But wherefore says she not she is unjust?
And wherefore say not I that I am old?
O, love's best habit is in seeming trust,
12 And age in love loves not to have years told.
     Therefore I lie with her, and she with me,
     And in our faults by lies we flattered be.

1 *truth* fidelity   3 *That* so that   7 *Simply* (1) foolishly (2)
pretending to be simple   7 *credit* believe   9 *unjust* unfaithful
11 *habit* appearance   11 *seeming trust* the appearance of truth
12 *told* counted   13 *lie with* (1) lie to (2) sleep with

139

O, call not me to justify the wrong
That thy unkindness lays upon my heart;
Wound me not with thine eye but with thy tongue;
Use power with power and slay me not by art.   *4*
Tell me thou lov'st elsewhere; but in my sight,
Dear heart, forbear to glance thine eye aside;
What need'st thou wound with cunning when thy
    might
Is more than my o'erpressed defense can bide?   *8*
Let me excuse thee; ah, my love well knows
Her pretty looks have been mine enemies,
And therefore from my face she turns my foes,
That they elsewhere might dart their injuries.   *12*
    Yet do not so; but since I am near slain,
    Kill me outright with looks and rid my pain.

---

4 *with power* i.e., openly, directly   4 *art* artful means   8 *o'er-
pressed* overpowered   11 *my foes* i.e., her looks

140

Be wise as thou art cruel; do not press
My tongue-tied patience with too much disdain,
Lest sorrow lend me words, and words express
4 The manner of my pity-wanting pain.
If I might teach thee wit, better it were,
Though not to love, yet love, to tell me so;
As testy sick men, when their deaths be near,
8 No news but health from their physicians know.
For if I should despair, I should grow mad,
And in my madness might speak ill of thee.
Now this ill-wresting world is grown so bad
12 Mad slanderers by mad ears believèd be.
    That I may not be so, nor thou belied,
    Bear thine eyes straight, though thy proud heart
        go wide.

1 *press* oppress 4 *manner* nature 4 *pity-wanting* unpitied
5 *wit* wisdom 6 *so* i.e., that you love me 7 *testy* fretful
11 *ill-wresting* i.e., misinterpreting everything for the worse
13 *so* (1) a "mad slanderer" (2) so believed 14 *wide* wide of
the mark

141

In faith I do not love thee with mine eyes,
For they in thee a thousand errors note;
But 'tis my heart that loves what they despise,
Who in despite of view is pleased to dote.   *4*
Nor are mine ears with thy tongue's tune delighted,
Nor tender feeling to base touches prone,
Nor taste, nor smell, desire to be invited
To any sensual feast with thee alone.   *8*
But my five wits nor my five senses can
Dissuade one foolish heart from serving thee,
Who leaves unswayed the likeness of a man,
Thy proud heart's slave and vassal wretch to be.   *12*
  Only my plague thus far I count my gain,
  That she that makes me sin awards me pain.

4 *Who in despite of view* which in spite of what they see   6 *base
touches* sexual contact   9 *But* but neither   9 *five wits* common
wit, imagination, fantasy, estimation, memory   10 *serving* loving
11 *Who . . . man* i.e., which ceases to rule and so leaves me what
is only the semblance of a man

142

Love is my sin, and thy dear virtue hate,
Hate of my sin, grounded on sinful loving.
O, but with mine compare thou thine own state,
4 And thou shalt find it merits not reproving,
Or if it do, not from those lips of thine,
That have profaned their scarlet ornaments
And sealed false bonds of love as oft as mine,
8 Robbed others' beds' revenues of their rents.
Be it lawful I love thee as thou lov'st those
Whom thine eyes woo as mine importune thee.
Root pity in thy heart, that, when it grows,
12 Thy pity may deserve to pitied be.
   If thou dost seek to have what thou dost hide,
   By self-example mayst thou be denied.

1 *dear* inmost   4 *it* i.e., my state   6 *scarlet ornaments* i.e., lips
(compared to scarlet wax that seals documents)   8 *Robbed*
. . . *rents* i.e., has robbed wives of what their husbands owed them
9 *Be it* let it be   13 *what* that which, i.e., pity

143

Lo, as a careful housewife runs to catch
One of her feathered creatures broke away,
Sets down her babe, and makes all swift dispatch
In pursuit of the thing she would have stay;   4
Whilst her neglected child holds her in chase,
Cries to catch her whose busy care is bent
To follow that which flies before her face,
Not prizing her poor infant's discontent: 8
So run'st thou after that which flies from thee,
Whilst I, thy babe, chase thee afar behind;
But if thou catch thy hope, turn back to me
And play the mother's part, kiss me, be kind.   12
　　So will I pray that thou mayst have thy *Will*,
　　If thou turn back and my loud crying still.

5 *holds her in chase* chases her   8 *prizing* regarding
13–14 Some scholarly follies are so extraordinary that they
deserve to be immortalized. Gregor Sarrazin, a German-Swiss,
emended these lines as follows:
So will I pray that thou may'est have thy *Hen,* (short for Henry)
If thou turn back and my loud crying pen.
　　　　　　　　　　　　　　　　　　W.H.A.

144

Two loves I have, of comfort and despair,
Which like two spirits do suggest me still;
The better angel is a man right fair,
4   The worser spirit a woman colored ill.
To win me soon to hell, my female evil
Tempteth my better angel from my side,
And would corrupt my saint to be a devil,
8   Wooing his purity with her foul pride.
And whether that my angel be turned fiend
Suspect I may, yet not directly tell;
But being both from me, both to each friend,
12   I guess one angel in another's hell.
        Yet this shall I ne'er know, but live in doubt,
        Till my bad angel fire my good one out.

1 *of comfort and despair* i.e., one offering heavenly mercy, the
other offering hellish despair   2 *suggest me still* always urge
me   4 *colored ill* i.e., dark   10 *directly* precisely   11 *from* away
from   11 *each* each other   12 *in another's hell* (with an allusion
to the female sexual organ)   14 *fire my good one out* i.e., com-
municate venereal disease

145

Those lips that Love's own hand did make
Breathed forth the sound that said, "I hate"
To me that languished for her sake.
But when she saw my woeful state,   *4*
Straight in her heart did mercy come,
Chiding that tongue that ever sweet
Was used in giving gentle doom,
And taught it thus anew to greet: *8*
"I hate," she altered with an end
That followed it as gentle day
Doth follow night, who, like a fiend,
From heaven to hell is flown away.   *12*
    "I hate" from hate away she threw,
    And saved my life, saying, "not you."

7 *doom* judgment   **9** *end* ending

146

Poor soul, the center of my sinful earth,
My sinful earth these rebel pow'rs that thee array,
Why dost thou pine within and suffer dearth,
4 Painting thy outward walls so costly gay?
Why so large cost, having so short a lease,
Dost thou upon thy fading mansion spend?
Shall worms, inheritors of this excess,
8 Eat up thy charge? Is this thy body's end?
Then, soul, live thou upon thy servant's loss,
And let that pine to aggravate thy store;
Buy terms divine in selling hours of dross;
12 Within be fed, without be rich no more:
  So shalt thou feed on Death, that feeds on men,
  And Death once dead, there's no more dying then.

1 *sinful earth* i.e., body   2 *My sinful earth* (obviously the printer mistakenly repeated here words of the previous line. Among suggested emendations are: "Thrall to," "Fooled by," "Rebuke," and "Leagued with")   4 *Painting* i.e., adorning   5 *cost* expense   7 *excess* extravagant expenditure   8 *charge* (1) expense (2) burden, i.e., the body   10 *that* i.e., the body   10 *aggravate* increase   11 *terms divine* ages of immortality

147

My love is as a fever, longing still
For that which longer nurseth the disease,
Feeding on that which doth preserve the ill,
Th' uncertain sickly appetite to please.   *4*
My reason, the physician to my love,
Angry that his prescriptions are not kept,
Hath left me, and I desperate now approve
Desire is death, which physic did except.   *8*
Past cure I am, now reason is past care,
And frantic-mad with evermore unrest;
My thoughts and my discourse as madmen's are,
At random from the truth vainly expressed: *12*
  For I have sworn thee fair, and thought thee
     bright,
  Who art as black as hell, as dark as night.

1 *still* always   **3** *preserve the ill* prolong the illness   **7–8** *approve*
. . . *except* find by experience that Desire, which refused med-
icine, is death (?)

148

O me, what eyes hath Love put in my head,
Which have no correspondence with true sight!
Or, if they have, where is my judgment fled,
4   That censures falsely what they see aright?
If that be fair whereon my false eyes dote,
What means the world to say it is not so?
If it be not, then love doth well denote
8   Love's eye is not so true as all men's no.
How can it? O, how can Love's eye be true,
That is so vexed with watching and with tears?
No marvel then though I mistake my view;
12   The sun itself sees not till heaven clears.
     O cunning Love, with tears thou keep'st me blind,
     Lest eyes well-seeing thy foul faults should find.

4 *censures* judges   8 *eye* (with a pun on "aye" in contrast with
all men's no)   10 *watching* wakefulness   11 *mistake my view*
err in what I see

149

Canst thou, O cruel, say I love thee not,
When I against myself with thee partake?
Do I not think on thee when I forgot
Am of myself, all tyrant for thy sake?   *4*
Who hateth thee that I do call my friend?
On whom frown'st thou that I do fawn upon?
Nay, if thou lour'st on me, do I not spend
Revenge upon myself with present moan?   *8*
What merit do I in myself respect
That is so proud thy service to despise,
When all my best doth worship thy defect,
Commanded by the motion of thine eyes?   *12*
    But, love, hate on, for now I know thy mind;
      Those that can see thou lov'st, and I am blind.

---

2 *partake* unite   3–4 *forgot/Am of* forget   4 *all tyrant* i.e., having become altogether a tyrant   8 *present moan* immediate grief
11 *defect* lack of good qualities

150

O, from what pow'r hast thou this pow'rful might
With insufficiency my heart to sway?
To make me give the lie to my true sight
4 And swear that brightness doth not grace the day?
Whence hast thou this becoming of things ill
That in the very refuse of thy deeds
There is such strength and warrantize of skill
8 That in my mind thy worst all best exceeds?
Who taught thee how to make me love thee more,
The more I hear and see just cause of hate?
O, though I love what others do abhor,
12 With others thou shouldst not abhor my state:
     If thy unworthiness raised love in me,
     More worthy I to be beloved of thee.

2 *insufficiency* unworthiness   2 *sway* rule   3 *give the lie to my true sight* accuse my true sight of lying   5 *becoming of things ill* i.e., power to make evil look attractive   7 *warrantize of skill* guarantee of mental power   13 *raised* (sexual innuendo?)

151

Love is too young to know what conscience is,
Yet who knows not conscience is born of love?
Then, gentle cheater, urge not my amiss,
Lest guilty of my faults thy sweet self prove.   *4*
For, thou betraying me, I do betray
My nobler part to my gross body's treason;
My soul doth tell my body that he may
Triumph in love; flesh stays no farther reason,   *8*
But, rising at thy name, doth point out thee,
As his triumphant prize. Proud of this pride,
He is contented thy poor drudge to be,
To stand in thy affairs, fall by thy side.   *12*
    No want of conscience hold it that I call
    Her "love" for whose dear love I rise and fall.

3 *urge not my amiss* stress not my sinfulness   **8** *flesh* the penis
8 *stays* awaits   **8** *reason* talk   **9** *rising* rebelling (with a sexual
pun, as in "point," line 9; "stand" and "fall," line 12; and "rise
and fall," line 14)   **10** *Proud of* swelling with

152

In loving thee thou know'st I am forsworn,
But thou art twice forsworn, to me love swearing;
In act thy bed-vow broke, and new faith torn
4 In vowing new hate after new love bearing.
But why of two oaths' breach do I accuse thee,
When I break twenty? I am perjured most,
For all my vows are oaths but to misuse thee,
8 And all my honest faith in thee is lost;
For I have sworn deep oaths of thy deep kindness,
Oaths of thy love, thy truth, thy constancy;
And, to enlighten thee, gave eyes to blindness,
12 Or made them swear against the thing they see;
    For I have sworn thee fair; more perjured eye,
    To swear against the truth so foul a lie.

1 *am forsworn* i.e., have broken (my marriage) vows 7 *but to misuse* merely to misrepresent 11 *enlighten thee* make you shine 11 *gave eyes to blindness* i.e., caused my eyes not to see the truth 13 *eye* eyes (with a pun on "I")

153

Cupid laid by his brand and fell asleep.
A maid of Dian's this advantage found,
And his love-kindling fire did quickly steep
In a cold valley-fountain of that ground;   4
Which borrowed from this holy fire of Love
A dateless lively heat, still to endure,
And grew a seething bath, which yet men prove
Against strange maladies a sovereign cure.   8
But at my mistress' eye Love's brand new-fired,
The boy for trial needs would touch my breast;
I, sick withal, the help of bath desired,
And thither hied, a sad distempered guest,   12
    But found no cure; the bath for my help lies
    Where Cupid got new fire—my mistress' eyes.

1 *brand* torch   2 *Dian* Diana, goddess of chastity   2 *advantage* opportunity   6 *dateless lively* eternal living   6 *still* always   7 *seething* boiling   7 *prove* find by experience   8 *sovereign* potent   10 *for trial needs would* as a test had to   11 *withal* with it   11 *bath* (possibly an allusion to the city of Bath, famous for its curative waters)   12 *distempered* diseased

154

The little Love-god lying once asleep
Laid by his side his heart-inflaming brand,
Whilst many nymphs that vowed chaste life to keep
4   Came tripping by, but in her maiden hand
The fairest votary took up that fire,
Which many legions of true hearts had warmed;
And so the general of hot desire
8   Was, sleeping, by a virgin hand disarmed.
This brand she quenchèd in a cool well by,
Which from Love's fire took heart perpetual,
Growing a bath and healthful remedy
12 For men diseased; but I, my mistress' thrall,
      Came there for cure, and this by that I prove:
      Love's fire heats water, water cools not love.

FINIS

1 *Love-god* Cupid   2 *brand* torch   5 *votary* one vowed to chastity   7 *general* leader, i.e., Cupid   12 *thrall* slave

Textual Note

The present text of the sonnets is based on the quarto of 1609, the only edition of any authority; all subsequent editions of the sonnets derive from that of 1609. Two of the sonnets (138 and 144) had been published, in slightly different versions, in a volume of poems entitled *The Passionate Pilgrim* (1599); quite possibly all or almost all of the sonnets were written in the middle '90s, though it is equally possible that some were written only shortly before Thorpe issued his quarto with 154 sonnets. There is no evidence that Shakespeare oversaw the publication; probably the order in which the sonnets are presented is the publisher's rather than the author's. In 1640 John Benson issued a second edition. He dropped Thorpe's dedication and eight sonnets, rearranged the order of the remaining ones, made numerous verbal changes to suggest that the sonnets were written to a woman and not to a man, and implied in a preface that the sonnets had never before been published.

The present edition keeps the arrangement of the 1609 quarto, but corrects obvious typographical errors and modernizes spelling and punctuation. Other departures from the quarto are listed below, the present reading first, in italics, and then the reading of the quarto, in roman.

The Textual Editor wishes to acknowledge his indebtedness, especially in the glosses, to his late teacher, Hyder Edward Rollins, whose indispensable *New Variorum Edition* is as likely as any scholarly book to bear it out to the edge of doom.

W.B.

12.4 *are* or　13.7 *Yourself* You selfe　19.3 *jaws* yawes　19.5 *fleets* fleet'st
25.9 *might* worth　26.12 *thy* their　27.10 *thy* their　34.12 *cross* losse
35.8 *thy . . . thy* their . . . their　41.8 *she* he　43.11 *thy* their　44.13
naught naughts　45.12 *thy* their　46.3 *thy* their　46.8 *thy* their　46.9
'cide side　46.14 *thy* their　47.11 *not* nor　50.6 *dully* duly　51.10 *perfect'st* perfects　55.1 *monuments* monument　56.13 *Or* As　65.12 *of* or
69.3 *due* end　69.5 *Thy* Their　70.1 *art* are　70.6 *Thy* Their　74.12 *remembered* remembred　76.7 *tell* fel　77.10 *blanks* blacks　90.11 *shall*
stall　91.8 *better* bitter　99.9 *One* Our　102.8 *her* his　111.1 *with* wish
112.14 *are* y'are　113.6 *latch* lack　113.14 *mine eye* mine　126.8 *minutes*
mynuit　128.11 *thy* their　128.14 *thy* their　129.11 *proved, a* proud and
132.6 *of the* of th'　132.9 *mourning* morning　138.12 *to have* t' haue
144.6 *side* sight　144.9 *fiend* finde　153.14 *eyes* eye

Commentaries

WILLIAM EMPSON

They That Have Power

[Sonnet 94]

I

It is agreed that *They that have power to hurt and will
do none* is a piece of grave irony, but there the matter is
generally left; you can work through all the notes in the
Variorum without finding out whether flower, lily, "owner,"
and person addressed are alike or opposed. One would like
to say that the poem has all possible such meanings, di-
gested into some order, and then try to show how this is
done, but the mere number of possible interpretations is
amusingly too great. Taking the simplest view (that any
two may be alike in some one property) any one of the
four either is or is not and either should or should not be
like each of the others; this yields 4096 possible move-
ments of thought, with other possibilities. The niggler is
routed here; one has honestly to consider what seems im-
portant.

From *Some Versions of Pastoral* by William Empson. London: Chatto
& Windus, Ltd., 1935; New York: New Directions, 1950. Reprinted by
permission of the publishers. All rights reserved.
  The two footnotes in this essay appear as errata in the original
edition.

"The best people are indifferent to temptation and de-
tached from the world; nor is this state selfish, because
they do good by unconscious influence, like the flower.
You must be like them; you are quite like them already.
But even the best people must be continually on their
guard, because they become the worst, just as the pure
and detached lily smells worst, once they fall from their
perfection"—("one's prejudice against them is only one's
consciousness of this fact"—the hint of irony in the poem
might be covered by this). It is a coherent enough Con-
fucian sentiment, and there is no very clear hint as to
irony in the words. No doubt *as stone* goes intentionally
too far for sympathy, and there is a suggestive gap in the
argument between octet and sestet, but one would not feel
this if it was Shakespeare's only surviving work.

There is no reason why the subtlety of the irony in so
complex a material must be capable of being pegged out
into verbal explanations. The vague and generalized lan-
guage of the descriptions, which might be talking about
so many sorts of people as well as feeling so many things
about them, somehow makes a unity like a crossroads,
which analysis does not deal with by exploring down the
roads; makes a solid flute on which you can play a multi-
tude of tunes, whose solidity no list of all possible tunes
would go far to explain. The balance of feeling is both very
complex and very fertile; experiences are recorded, and
metaphors invented, in the Sonnets, which he went on
"applying" as a dramatist, taking particular cases of them
as if they were wide generalizations, for the rest of his life.
One can't expect, in writing about such a process, to say
anything very tidy and complete.

But one does not start interpreting out of the void, even
though the poem once partly interpreted seems to stand
on its own. If this was Shakespeare's only surviving work
it would still be clear, supposing one knew about the other
Elizabethans, that it involves somehow their feelings about
the Machiavellian, the wicked plotter who is exciting and
civilized and in some way right about life; which seems an
important though rather secret element in the romance that
Shakespeare extracted from his patron. In any case one

has only to look at the sonnets before and after it to be
sure that it has some kind of irony. The one before is full
of fear and horror at the hypocrisy he is so soon to recom-
mend; and yet it is already somehow cuddled, as if in
fascination or out of a refusal to admit that it was there.

> So shall I liue, supposing thou art true,
> Like a deceiued husband, . . .
> For ther can liue no hatred in thine eye
> Therefore in that I cannot know thy change, . . .
> How like *Eaues* apple doth thy beauty grow,
> If thy sweet vertue answere not thy show.

So the *summer's flower* may be its apple-blossom. His
virtue is still sweet, whether he has any or not; the clash
of fact with platonic idealism is too fearful to be faced
directly. In the sonnet after, with a blank and exhausted
humility, it has been faced; there remains for the expres-
sion of his love, in the least flaunting of poetry, the voice
of caution.

> How sweet and louely dost thou make the shame, . . .
> Take heed (deare heart) of this large privilege.

The praise of hypocrisy is in a crucial and precarious
condition of balance between these two states of mind.

The root of the ambivalence, I think, is that W. H. is
loved as an arriviste, for an impudent worldliness that
Shakespeare finds shocking and delightful. The reasons
why he treated his poet badly are the same as the reasons
why he was fascinating, which gives its immediate point
to the profound ambivalence about the selfishness of the
flower. Perhaps he is like the cold person in his hardness
and worldly judgment, not in his sensuality and generosity
of occasional impulse; like the flower in its beauty, vulnera-
bility, tendency to excite thoughts about the shortness of
life, self-centeredness, and power in spite of it to give
pleasure, not in its innocence and fertility; but the irony
may make any of these change over. Both owner and flower
seem self-centered and inscrutable, and the cold person is
at least like the lily in that it is symbolically chaste, but the

summer's flower, unlike the lily, seems to stand for the full life of instinct. It is not certain that the owner is liable to fester as the lily is—Angelo did, but W. H. is usually urged to acquire the virtues of Angelo. Clearly there is a jump from octet to sestet; the flower is not like the owner in its solitude and its incapacity to hurt or simulate; it might be because of this that it is of a summer only and may fester; yet we seem chiefly meant to hold W. H. in mind and take them as parallel. As for punctuation, the only full stop is at the end; all lines have commas after them except the fourth, eighth, and twelfth, which have colons.

> They that haue powre to hurt, and will doe none,
> That doe not do the thing, they most do showe,
> Who mouing others, are themselves as stone,
> Vnmoued, could, and to temptation slow:

They may *show,* while hiding the alternative, for the first couplet, the power to hurt or the determination not to hurt—cruelty or mercy, for the second, the strength due to chastity or to sensual experience, for either, a reckless or cautious will, and the desire for love or for control; all whether they are stealers of hearts or of public power. They are a very widespread group; we are only sure at the end that some kind of hypocrisy has been advised and threatened.

> They rightly do inherit heavens graces,
> And husband natures ritches from expence,

Either "inherit, they alone, by right" or "inherit what all men inherit and use it rightly"; these correspond to the opposed views of W. H. as aristocrat and vulgar careerist. There is a similar range of idea, half hidden by the pretense of easy filling of the form, in the pun on *graces* and shift to *riches. Heaven's graces* may be prevenient grace (strength from God to do well), personal graces which seem to imply heavenly virtues (the charm by which you deceive people), or merely God's gracious gift of *nature's riches;* which again may be the personal graces, or the strength and taste which make him capable either of "up-holding his house" or of taking his pleasure, or merely the actual wealth of which he is an *owner*. Clearly this gives plenty of room for irony in the statement that the cold people, with their fine claims, do well all round; it also conveys "I am seeing you as a whole; I am seeing these things as necessary rather than as your fault."

> They are the Lords and owners of their faces,
> Others, but stewards of their excellence:

It may be their beauty they put to their own uses, high or low, or they may just have poker faces; this gives the same range of statement. The capital which tends to isolate *lords* from its phrase suggests "they are the only true aristocrats; if you are not like them you should not pretend to be one." *Others* may be stewards of their own excellence (in contrast with *faces*—"though they are enslaved they may be better and less superficial than the cold people") or of the cold people's excellence (with a suggestion of "Their Excellencies"); the less plausible sense is insisted on by the comma after *others*. This repeats the doubt about how far the cold people are really excellent, and there may be a hint of a doubt about how far the individual is isolated, which anticipates the metaphor of the flower. And "stewards of their own excellence" may be like "stewards of the buttery" or like "stewards of a certain lord"; either "the good things they have do good to others, not to them" (they are too generous; I cannot ask you to aim so high in virtue, because I desire your welfare, not other people's, and indeed because you wouldn't do it anyway) or "they are under the power of their own impulses, which are good things so long as they are not in power" (they are deceived; acts caused by weakness are not really generous at all). Yet this may be the condition of the flower and the condition for fullness of life; you cannot know beforehand what life will bring you if you open yourself to it, and certainly the flower does not; it is because they are unnatural and unlike flowers that the cold people rule nature, and the cost may be too great.

Or the flower and the cold person may be two unlike examples of the limitation necessary to success, one experienced in its own nature, the other in the world; both, the irony would imply, are in fact *stewards*.

There is a Christian parable at work in both octet and sestet; in the octet that of the talents. You will not be forgiven for hoarding your talents; some sort of success is demanded; you must at least use your powers to the full even if for your own squalid purpose. The pain and wit and solemnity of *rightly*, its air of summing up a long argument, depend on the fact that these metaphors have been used to recommend things to W. H. before.

> Natures bequest giues nothing but doth lend,
> And being franck she lends to those are free:
>
> Who lets so faire a house fall to decay,
> Which husbandry in honour might uphold,

Rightly to be free with yourself, in the first simple paradox, was the best saving of yourself (you should put your money into marriage and a son); it is too late now to advise that, or to say it without being sure to be understood wrongly (this is 94; the first sonnet about his taking Shakespeare's mistress is 40); the advice to be generous as natural has become the richer but more contorted advice to be like the flower. Rightly to husband nature's riches, earlier in the sequence, was to accept the fact that one is only steward of them;

> Thou that are now the worlds fresh ornament,
> And only herauld to the gaudy spring,
> Within thine owne bud buriest thy content,
> And tender chorle makst waste in niggarding:

the flower was wrong to live to itself alone, and would become a tottered weed (2) whether it met with infection or not.

Though indeed *husbandry* is still recommended; it is not the change of opinion that has so much effect but the use of the same metaphors with a shift of feeling in them. The legal metaphors (debts to nature and so forth) used for the loving complaint that the man's chastity was selfish are still used when he becomes selfish in his debauchery; Shakespeare's own notation here seems to teach him; the more curiously because the metaphors were used so flatly in the earliest sonnets (1, 2, 4, 6, then 13; not again till now), only formally urging marriage, and perhaps written to order. It is like using a mathematical identity which implies a proof about a particular curve and then finding that it has a quite new meaning if you take the old constants as variables. It is these metaphors that have grown, till they involve relations between a man's powers and their use, his nature and his will, the individual and the society, which could be applied afterwards to all human circumstances.

> The sommers flowre is to the sommer sweet,
> Though to it selfe, it onely liue and die,

The use of *the* summer's flower about a human being is enough to put it at us that the flower will die by the end of summer, that the man's life is not much longer, and that the pleasures of the creature therefore cannot be despised for what they are. *Sweet to the summer* (said of the flower), since the summer is omnipresent and in a way Nature herself, may mean "sweet to God" (said of the man); or may mean "adding to the general sweetness; sweet to everybody that comes across it in its time." It may do good to others though not by effort or may simply be a good end in itself (or combining these, may only be able to do good by concentrating on itself as an end); a preparatory evasion of the central issue about egotism.

Either "though it lives only for itself" or "though, in its own opinion, so far as it can see, it does no more than live and die." In the first it is a rose, extravagant and doing good because the public likes to see it flaunting; in the second a violet, humble and doing good in private through an odor of sanctity. It is the less plausible sense which is insisted on by the comma after *itself*. Or you may well say that the flower is neither, but the final lily; the whole passage is hinting at the lilies of the field like whom Solomon was not arrayed.

This parable itself combines what the poem so ingeniously keeps on combining; the personal power of beauty and the political power of wisdom; so as to imply that the political power has in itself a sort of beauty and the personal beauty, however hollow it may be, a sort of moral grandeur through power. But in England "consider the lilies of the field," were we not at once told of their glory, would suggest lilies-of-the-valley; that name indeed occurs in the Song of Solomon, in surprising correspondence to the obviously grandiose Rose of Sharon. Shakespeare, I think, had done what the inventor of the name must have done, had read into the random flower names of the Bible the same rich clash of suggestion—an implied mutual comparison that elevates both parties—as he makes here between the garden flower and the wild flower. The first sense (the rose) gives the root idea—"a brilliant aristocrat like you gives great pleasure by living as he likes; for such a person the issue of selfishness does not arise"; this makes W. H. a Renaissance Magnificent Man, combining all the virtues with a many-sidedness like that of these phrases about him. The unlikeness of the cold people and the flowers, if you accept them as like, then implies "man is not placed like flowers and though he had best imitate them may be misled in doing so; the Machiavellian is much more really like the flower than the Swain is." And yet there is a suggestion in the comparison to the flower (since only beauty is demanded of it—Sonnet 54 made an odd and impermanent attempt at quelling this doubt by equating truth with scent) that W. H. has only power to keep up an air of reconciling in himself the inconsistent virtues, or even of being a Machiavellian about the matter, and that it is this that puts him in danger like the flower. Or however genuine he may be he is pathetic; such a man is all too "natural"; there is no need to prop up our ideas about him with an aristocratic "artificial" flower. So this class-centered praise is then careful half to hide itself by adding the second sense and the humble flower, and this leads it to a generalization: "all men do most good to others by fulfilling their own natures." Full as they are of Christian echoes, the Sonnets are concerned with an idea strong enough to be balanced against Christianity; they state the opposite to the idea of self-sacrifice.

But the machinery of the statement is peculiar; its clash of admiration and contempt seems dependent on a clash of feeling about the classes. One might connect it with that curious trick of pastoral which for extreme courtly flattery—perhaps to give self-respect to both poet and patron, to show that the poet is not ignorantly easy to impress, nor the patron to flatter—writes about the poorest people; and with those jazz songs which give an intense effect of luxury and silk underwear by pretending to be about slaves naked in the fields. To those who care chiefly about biography this trick must seem monstrously tantalizing; Wilde built the paradox of his essay on it, and it is true that Shakespeare might have set the whole thing to work from the other end about a highly trained mudlark brought in to act his princesses. But it is the very queerness of the trick that makes it so often useful in building models of the human mind; and yet the power no less than the universality of this poem depends on generalizing the trick so completely as to seem independent of it.

> But if that flowre with base infection meete,
> The basest weed out-braues his dignity:
>> For sweetest things turn sowrest by their deedes,
>> Lilies that fester, smell far worse than weeds.

It is not clear how the metaphor from "meet" acts; it may be like "meet with disaster"—"if it catches infection, which would be bad luck," or like meeting someone in the street, as most men do safely—"*any* contact with infection is fatal to so peculiarly placed a creature." The first applies to the natural and unprotected flower, the second to the lily that has the hubris and fate of greatness. They are not of course firmly separated, but *lilies* are separated from the *flower* by a colon and an intervening generalization, whereas the flower is only separated from the cold people (not all of whom need be lilies) by a colon; certainly the flower as well as the lily is in danger, but this does not make them identical and equal to W. H. The neighboring sonnets continually say that his deeds can do nothing to destroy his sweetness, and this seems to make the terrible last line point at him somewhat less directly. One may indeed take it as "Though so debauched, you keep your looks. Only mean people who never give themselves heartily to anything can do that. But the best hypocrite is found out in the end, and shown as the worst." But Shakespeare may also be congratulating W. H. on an imperfection which acts as a preservative; he is a son of the world and can protect himself, like the cold people, or a spontaneous and therefore fresh sinner, like the flower; he may safely stain, as heaven's sun, the kisser of carrion, staineth. At any rate it is not of virginity, at this stage, that he can be accused. The smell of a big lily is so lush and insolent, suggests so powerfully both incense and pampered flesh—the traditional metaphor about it is so perfect—that its festering can only be that due to the hubris of spirituality; it is ironically generous to apply it to the careerist to whom hypocrisy is recommended; and yet in the fact that we seem meant to apply it to him there is a glance backwards, as if to justify him, at the ambition involved in even the most genuine attempt on heaven. You may say that Shakespeare dragged in the last line as a quotation from *Edward III* that doesn't quite fit; it is also possible that (as often happens to poets, who tend to make in their lives a situation they have already written about) he did not till now see the full width of its application.

In a sense the total effect is an evasion of Shakespeare's problem; it gives him a way of praising W. H. in spite of anything. In the flower the oppositions are transcended; it is because it is self-concentrated that it has so much to give and because it is undesigning that it is more grandiose in beauty than Solomon. But it is held in mind chiefly for comfort; none of the people suggested to us are able to imitate it very successfully; nor if they could would they be safe. Yet if W. H. has festered, that at least makes him a lily, and at least not a stone; if he is not a lily, he is in the less danger of festering.

I must try to sum up the effect of so complex an irony, half by trying to follow it through a gradation. "I am praising to you the contemptible things you admire, you little plotter; this is how the others try to betray you through flattery; yet it is your little generosity, though it show only as lewdness, which will betray you; for it is wise to be cold, both because you are too inflammable and because I have been so much hurt by you who are heartless; yet I can the better forgive you through that argument from our common isolation; I must praise to you your very faults, especially your selfishness, because you can only now be safe by cultivating them further; yet this is the most dangerous of necessities; people are greedy for your fall as for that of any of the great; indeed no one can rise above common life, as you have done so fully, without in the same degree sinking below it; you have made this advice real to me, because I cannot despise it for your sake; I am only sure that you are valuable and in danger."

II

One may point out that the reason so little can be deduced about W. H., the reason that Butler and Wilde (though he had so much sympathy for snobbery) could make a plausible case for his being not a patron but an actor, is that this process of interaction between metaphors, which acts like a generalization, is always carried so far; the contradictory elements in the relation are brought out and opposed absolutely, so that we cannot know their proportions in real life. It is hard not to go off down one of the roads at the crossing, and get one plain meaning for the poem from that, because Shakespeare himself did that so very effectively afterwards; a part of the situation of the Sonnets, the actual phrases designed for it, are given to Prince Henry, to Angelo, to Troilus, to the Greek army; getting further from the original as time went on. I shall look at the first two. It is only partly true that this untidy process, if successful, might tell one more about the original situation; discoveries of language and feeling made from a personal situation may develop themselves so that they can be applied to quite different dramatic situations; but to know about these might tell one more about the original discoveries. The fact that the feelings in this sonnet could be used for such different people as Angelo and Prince Henry, different both in their power and their coldness, is an essential part of its breadth.

The crucial first soliloquy of Prince Henry was put in to save his reputation with the audience; it is a willful destruction of his claims to generosity, indeed to honesty, if only in Falstaff's sense; but this is not to say that it was a mere job with no feeling behind it. It was a concession to normal and decent opinion rather than to the groundlings; the man who was to write *Henry V* could feel the force of that as well as take care of his plot; on the other hand, it cannot have been written without bitterness against the prince. It was probably written about two years after the second, more intimate dedication to Southampton, and is almost a cento from the Sonnets.

We would probably find the prince less puzzling if Shakespeare had rewritten *Henry VI* in his prime. The theme at the back of the series, after all, is that the Henries are usurpers; however great the virtues of Henry V may be, however rightly the nation may glory in his deeds, there is something fishy about him and the justice of Heaven will overtake his son. In having some sort of double attitude to the prince Shakespeare was merely doing his work as a history writer. For the critic to drag in a personal situation from the Sonnets is neither an attack nor a justification; it claims only to show where the feelings the play needed were obtained.

Sir Walter Raleigh said that the play was written when Shakespeare was becoming successful and buying New Place, so that he became interested in the problems of successful people like Henries IV and V rather than in poetical failures like Richard II. On this view we are to see in Prince Henry the Swan himself; he has made low friends only to get local color out of them, and now drops them with a bang because he has made money and grand friends. It is possible enough, though I don't know why it was thought

pleasant; anyway such a personal association is far at the
back of the mind and one would expect several to be at
work together. Henry might carry a grim externalization
of self-contempt as well as a still half-delighted reverbera-
tion of Southampton; Falstaff an attack on some rival play-
wright or on Florio as tutor of Southampton as well as a
savage and joyous externalization of self-contempt. But I
think only the second of these alternatives fits in with the
language and echoes a serious personal situation. Henry's
soliloquy demands from us just the sonnets' mood of bitter
complaisance; the young man must still be praised and
loved, however he betrays his intimates, because we see
him all shining with the virtues of success. So I shall now
fancy Falstaff as Shakespeare (he has obviously some great
forces behind him) and Henry as the patron who has re-
cently betrayed him.

> I know you all, and will a-while vphold
> The vnyoak'd humor of your idlenesse:
> Yet heerein will I imitate the Sunne,
> Who doth permit the base contagious cloudes
> To smother vp his Beauty from the world,
> That when he please again to be himselfe,
> Being wanted, he may be more wondred at,
> By breaking through the foule and vgly mists
> Of vapours, that did seeme to strangle him.

This seems quite certainly drawn from the earliest and
most pathetic of the attempts to justify W. H.

> Fvll many a glorious morning haue I seene, . . .
> Anon permit the *basest cloudes* to ride, . . .
> With *ougly* rack on his celestiall face, . . .
>   *Suns* of the world may staine, when heauens sun staineth.

But it is turned backwards; the sun is now to free itself
from the clouds by the very act of betrayal. "Oh that you
were yourself" (13) and "have eyes to wonder" (106) are
given the same twist into humility; Shakespeare admits,
with Falstaff in front of him, that the patron would be
better off without friends in low life. The next four lines,

developing the idea that you make the best impression on
people by only treating them well at rare intervals, are a
prosaic rehash of "Therefore are feasts so solemn and so
rare," etc. (52); what was said of the policy of the friend
is now used for the policy of the politician, though in both
play and sonnet they are opposed. The connection in the
next lines is more doubtful.

> So when this loose behaviour I throw off
> And pay the debt I never promised
> By so much better than my word I am
> By so much shall I falsify men's hopes

(He does indeed, by just so much.) This *debt* looks like
an echo of the debt to nature there was so much doubt
about W. H.'s method of paying; it has turned into a debt
to society. At any rate in the sonnetlike final couplet

> I'll so offend, to make offense a skill

("The tongue that tells the story of thy days . . . Cannot
dispraise but in a kind of praise") we have the central
theme of all the sonnets of apology; the only difference,
though it is a big one, is that this man says it about himself.

One element at least in this seems to reflect a further
doubt onto the sonnet I have considered; the prince may
be showing by this soliloquy that he can avoid infection,
or may be an example of how sour a lord and owner can
turn in his deeds on Coronation Day. The last irony and
most contorted generosity one can extract from the sonnet
is in the view that Shakespeare himself is the basest weed,
that to meet him is to meet infection, that the result of be-
ing faithful to his friendship would be to be outbraved even
by him, that the advice to be a cold person and avoid the
fate of the lily is advice to abandon Shakespeare once for all.

This interpretation is more than once as firmly contra-
dicted by Falstaff as it will be by my readers. He first comes
on in a great fuss about his good name; he has been rated
in the streets for leading astray Harry. At the end of the
scene we find that this was unfair to him; the prince makes

clear by the soliloquy that he is well able to look after himself. Meanwhile Falstaff amuses himself by turning the accusation the other way round.

> O, thou hast damnable iteration, and art indeede able to corrupt a Saint. Thou hast done much harme unto me *Hal*, God forgiue thee for it. Before I knew thee *Hal*, I knew nothing: and now I am (if a man shold speake truly) little better than one of the wicked. I must giue ouer this life, and I will giue it over: and I do not, I am a Villaine. Ile be damn'd for never a Kings sonne in Christendome.
>
> PRIN. Where shall we take a purse to morrow, Iacke?

The audience were not expected to believe this aspect of the matter, but there may well be some truth in it if applied to the situation Shakespeare had at the back of his mind. The other aspect is also preserved for us in the Sonnets.

> I may not euer-more acknowledge thee,
> Least my bewailed guilt should do thee shame,
> Nor thou with publike kindnesse honour me,
> Unlesse thou take that honour from thy name:

"I not only warn you against bad company; I admit I am part of it." One could throw in here that letter about Southampton wasting his time at the playhouse and out of favor with the Queen.

There are two sums of a thousand pounds concerned, so that the phrase is kept echoing through both parts of the history; it seems to become a symbol of Falstaff's hopes and his betrayal. The first he got by the robbery at Gadshill, and the prince at once robbed him of it; supposedly to give back to its owner, if you take his reluctance to steal seriously, but we hear no more of that.[1] He says he will give it to Francis the drawer, and Falstaff pacifies the hostess by saying he will get it back.

---

[1] The prince does say he has given the money back (III.iii.177), so this is a mistake; but one is free to suspect that he wouldn't have done it unless threatened by exposure.

Part I, III. iii.

> HOSTESS. . . . . and sayde this other day, You ought him
> a thousand pound.
> PRINCE. Sirrah, do I owe you a thousand pound?
> FALSTAFF. A thousand pound *Hal?* A Million. Thy loue
> is worth a Million: thou ow'st me thy loue.

He will pay neither. But Falstaff gets another thousand
pounds from Shallow, and the phrase is all he clings to in
the riddling sentence at his final discomfiture: "Master
Shallow, I owe you a thousand pound." This is necessary,
to seem calm and reassure Shallow; it is either a sweeping
gesture of renunciation ("What use to me now is the
money I need never have repaid to this fool?") or a com-
fort since it reminds him that he has got the money and
certainly won't repay it; but it is meant also for the king
to hear and remember ("I class you with Shallow and the
rest of my friends"). I cannot help fancying an obscure
connection between this sum and the thousand pounds
which, we are told, Southampton once gave Shakespeare,
to go through with a purchase that he had a mind to.

It is as well to look at Falstaff in general for a moment,
to show what this tender attitude to him has to fit in with.
The plot treats him as a simple Punch, whom you laugh
at with good humor, though he is wicked, because he is
always knocked down and always bobs up again. (Our atti-
tude to him as a Character entirely depends on the Plot,
and yet he is a Character who very nearly destroyed the
Plot as a whole.) People sometimes take advantage of this
to view him as a lovable old dear; a notion which one can
best refute by considering him as an officer.

Part I. v. iii.

> I haue led my rag of Muffins where they are pepper'd:
> there's not three of my 150 left alive, and they for the
> Townes end, to beg during life.

We saw him levy a tax in bribes on the men he left; he
now kills all the weaklings he conscripted, in order to keep

their pay. A large proportion of the groundlings consisted
of disbanded soldiers who had suffered under such a sys-
tem; the laughter was a roar of hatred here; he is "comic"
like a miracle-play Herod. (Whereas Harry has no quali-
ties that are obviously not W. H.'s.) And yet it is out of
his defense against this, the least popularizable charge
against him, that he makes his most unanswerable retort
to the prince.

> PRINCE. Tell me, Jack, whose fellows are these that
> come after?
> FAL. Mine, Hal, mine.
> PRINCE. I never did see such pitiful rascals.
> FAL. Tut, tut; good enough to toss; food for powder,
> food for powder; they'll fill a pit as well as better; tush,
> man, mortal men, mortal men.

Mortal conveys both "all men are in the same boat, all
equal before God" and "all you want is slaughter." No
one in the audience was tempted to think Harry as wicked
as his enemy Hotspur, who deserved death as much as Lear
for wanting to divide England. But this remark needed to
be an impudent cover for villainy if the strength of mind
and heart in it were not to be too strong, to make the squab-
bles of ambitious and usurping persons too contemptible.

On the other hand, Falstaff's love for the prince is cer-
tainly meant as a gap in his armor; one statement (out of
so many) of this comes where the prince is putting his life
in danger and robbing him of the (stolen) thousand pounds.

> I haue forsworne his company hourely any time this
> two and twenty yeares, and yet I am bewitcht with the
> Rogues company. If the Rascal haue not giuen me
> medecines to make me loue him,[2] Ile be hang'd; it could
> not be else; I haue drunke Medecines.

He could continually be made to say such things without
stopping the laugh at him, partly because one thinks he is

2 This is a mistake; it must be Poins whom Falstaff accuses of
administering the love philter. But I think Falstaff is drawn as regularly
expressing love for young men who rob for him, without complete in-
sincerity, and as being unusually sincere in the case of the prince.

pretending love to the prince for his own interest; "never any man's thought keeps the roadway" as well as those of the groundlings who think him a hypocrite about it, but this phrase of mockery at them is used only to dignify the prince; the more serious Falstaff's expression of love becomes the more comic it is, whether as hopeless or as hypocrisy. But to stretch one's mind round the whole character (as is generally admitted) one must take him, though as the supreme expression of the cult of mockery as strength and the comic idealization of freedom, yet as both villainous and tragically ill-used.

Angelo is further from the Sonnets than Henry both in date and situation; he is merely an extreme, perhaps not very credible, example of the cold person and the lily; both simply as chaste and as claiming to be more than human, which involves being at least liable to be as much less. He has odd connections with this sonnet through *Edward III*, which may help to show that there is a real connection of ideas. In the following lines he is recoiling with horror from the idea that Isabella has been using her virtue as a temptation for him, which was just what her brother expected her to do (I. ii. 185—she is a cold person but can "move men").

II. ii. 165–168.

> Not she: nor doth she tempt; but it is I,
> That, lying by the Violet in the Sunne,
> Doe as the Carrion do's, not as the flowre,
> Corrupt with vertuous season:

Edward III is also a man in authority tempting a chaste woman, and he too uses the notion that her qualities are a temptation, so that it is half her fault.

II. i. 58.

> the queen of beauty's queens shall see
> Herself the ground of my infirmity.

Both Angelo's metaphor and the chief line of this sonnet come from a speech by the lady's father, which contains the germ of most of the ideas we are dealing with.

II. i. 430–457.

> The greater man, the greater is the thing,
> Be it good or bad, that he shall undertake . . .
> The freshest summer's day doth soonest taint
> The loathed carrion that it seems to kiss . . .
> Lillies that fester smell far worse than weeds;
> And every glory that inclines to sin,
> The shame is treble by the opposite.

The freshest summer's day is always likely to kiss carrion, and the suggestion from this is that the great man is always likely to do great harm as well as great good. The sun kissing carrion is brought out again both for Falstaff and by Hamlet (1 *Henry IV*, II. iv. 113; *Hamlet*, II. ii. 158); it is clear that the complex of metaphor in this speech, whether Shakespeare wrote it or not, developed afterwards as a whole in his mind.

The obvious uses of the language of the Sonnets about Angelo all come in the first definition of his character by the Duke; once started like this he goes off on his own. The fascination of the irony of the passage is that it applies to Angelo's incorruptible virtues, associated with his chastity, the arguments and metaphors which had been used to urge abrogation of chastity on W. H.; nor is this irrelevant to the play. As in *virtues, torches*, and *fine touches*, its language, here and throughout, is always perversely on the edge of a bawdy meaning; even *belongings* may have a suggestion, helped out by "longings," of nature's gift of desire. It seems impossible even to praise the good qualities of Angelo without bringing into the hearer's mind those other good qualities that Angelo refuses to recognize. The most brilliant example of this trick in the play is the continual pun on *sense*, for sensuality, sensibleness (which implies the claim of Lucio) and sensibility (which implies a further claim of the poet). The first use may be unequivocal, as if to force the sexual meaning on our notice.

I. iv. 59   The wanton stings, and motions of the
                             sence.

II. ii. 141. ANGELO. Shee speakes, and 'tis such sence
                That my sence breeds with it; fare you
                    well.

II. ii. 168.   Can it be
                That Modesty may more betray our Sence
                Than womans lightnesse?

II. iv. 73.   Nay, but heare me.
                Your sence pursues not mine: either you
                  are ignorant,
                Or seeme so craft(il)y; and that's not good.

IV. iv. 27.   He should haue liu'd,
                Save that his riotous youth with dangerous
                  sence,
                Might in the times to come have ta'en
                  revenge.

V. i. 225. MARIANA. As there is sence in truth, and truth in
                  vertue,
                I am affianced this man's wife, as strongly
                As words could make vp vowes:

But this sort of thing does not depend on echoes from the Sonnets, and I think those that occur have a further effect.

> Thy selfe, and thy belongings
> Are not thine owne so proper, as to waste
> Thy selfe upon thy vertues; they on thee:
> Heauen doth with us, as we, with Torches doe,
> Not light them for themselves: For if our vertues
> Did not goe forth of us, 'twere all alike
> As if we had them not: Spirits are not finely touch'd,
> But to fine issues: nor nature never lends
> The smallest scruple of her excellence,
> But like a thrifty goddesse, she determines
> Her selfe the glory of a creditour,
> Both thanks, and vse;

"All are but stewards of her excellence"—indeed *their* in the sonnet might refer back to *nature's riches*. Even Angelo is wrong to think he can be a lord and owner, though he seems the extreme case of those capable of reserve and power. He is a *torch* whom nature tricks because she destroys it by making it brilliant; it was because he accepted office and prepared to use his virtues that she could trick him all but disastrously into using more of them than he intended. For "virtues" mean both "good qualities" and "capacities" ("a dormitive virtue") whether for good or ill; the same ambivalent attitude both towards worldly goods and towards what claim to be spiritual goods is conveyed by this as by the clash between *heaven's graces* and *nature's riches*. The same pun and irony on it, with a hint of a similar movement of thought about *honor,* are used when Isabella takes leave of Angelo after her first interviews.

II. ii. 162–164. Isab. Saue your Honor.
           Ang. From thee: euen from thy vertue.
               What's this? what's this? is this her fault, or mine?
               The Tempter, or the Tempted, who sins most?

It is his virtues and Isabella's between them that both trick him and nearly destroy Claudio. Not of course that this is straightforward satire against virtue in the sense of chastity; the first great speech of Claudio about "too much liberty" has all the weight and horror of the lust sonnet (129) from which it is drawn; only the still greater mockery of Claudio could so drag the play back to its attack on Puritanism.

The issue indeed is more general than the sexual one; it is "liberty, my Lucio, liberty," as Claudio makes clear at once; which runs through pastoral and is at the heart of the clowns. (Lawrence too seems to make sex the type of liberty; Shaw's Don Juan liberty the type of sex.) "Nature in general is a cheat, and all those who think themselves owners are pathetic." Yet we seem here to transfer to Nature the tone of bitter complaisance taken up towards W. H. when he seemed an owner; she now, as he was, must be given the benefit of the doubt inseparable from these shifting phrases; she too must be let rob you by tricks and still be worshiped. There is the same suggestion with the same metaphors in that splendid lecture to Achilles to make him use his virtues as a fighter further; whether rightly to *thank* her is to view yourself as an owner or a steward, you must still in the end pay her the compound interest on her gifts, and still keep up the pretense that they are free. This tone of generous distaste for the conditions of life, which gives the play one of its few suggestions of sympathy for Angelo, I think usually goes with a suggestion of the Sonnets. For instance, it is the whole point about Bassanio; more than any other suitor he is an arriviste loved only for success and seeming; his one merit, and it is enough, is to recognize this truth with Christian humility. His speech before the caskets about the falsity of seeming is full of phrases from the Sonnets (e.g. 68, about hair) and may even have a dim reference to the Dark Lady. It is not surprising that this sentiment should make Shakespeare's mind hark back to the Sonnets, because it was there so essential; these poems of idealization of a patron and careerist depend upon it for their strength and dignity. "Man is so placed that the sort of thing you do is in degree all that anyone can do; success does not come from mere virtue, and without some external success a virtue is not real even to itself. One must not look elsewhere; success of the same nature as yours is all that the dignity, whether of life or poetry, can be based upon." This queer sort of realism, indeed, is one of the main things he had to say.

The feeling that life is essentially inadequate to the human spirit, and yet that a good life must avoid saying so, is naturally at home with most versions of pastoral; in pastoral you take a limited life and pretend it is the full and normal one, and a suggestion that one must do this with all life, because the normal is itself limited, is easily put into the trick though not necessary to its power. Conversely any expression of the idea that all life is limited may be regarded as only a trick of pastoral, perhaps chiefly intended to hold all our attention and sympathy for some limited life, though again this is not necessary to it either on grounds of truth or beauty; in fact the suggestion of pastoral may be only a protection for the idea which must at last be taken alone. The business of interpretation is obviously very complicated. Literary uses of the problem of free will and necessity, for example, may be noticed to give curiously bad arguments and I should think get their strength from keeping you in doubt between the two methods. Thus Hardy is fond of showing us an unusually stupid person subjected to very unusually bad luck, and then a moral is drawn, not merely by inference but by solemn assertion, that we are all in the same boat as this person whose story is striking precisely because it is unusual. The effect may be very grand, but to make an otherwise logical reader accept the process must depend on giving him obscure reasons for wishing it so. It is clear at any rate that this grand notion of the inadequacy of life, so various in its means of expression, so reliable a bass note in the arts, needs to be counted as a possible territory of pastoral.

HALLETT SMITH

from *Elizabethan Poetry*

Some of the most impressive and eloquent of the sonnets are those which depend less upon a reflective situation for their framework than upon an apparent display of the poet's moods directly. It is especially true that, of these sonnets, those expressing a mood of despair or disillusion, of melancholy over the failure of the world or of the human personality, remind us of passages in the tragedies. The ideas are sometimes bitter in the manner of a Hamlet or a Lear. The motivation seems to be partly the same motivation that lies behind the satire of the 1590s, partly a more profound sense of the inevitable corruption of man in a world which is beyond his managing or even his understanding. Hamlet's awareness of the reasons for rejecting the world is reflected in No. 66, "Tir'd with all these, for restful death I cry." Yet the main burden of these sonnets of despondency is not that the fault lies in a corrupting world; they throw the principal emphasis upon the truant disposition of the speaker himself; that is to say, on the face of it they seem more psychological than satirical. Two of the most effective of these sonnets of mood are Nos. 29 and 30, "When in disgrace with fortune and men's eyes" and "When to the sessions of sweet silent thought."

Shakespeare's method in these sonnets may best be observed in No. 73. Here the professed subject is the poet's age, which is contrasted with the youth of the young man addressed in several other sonnets. But the resultant mood is the same mood of despair as that of the sonnets we have

From *Elizabethan Poetry: A Study in Conventions, Meaning, and Expression* by Hallett Smith. Cambridge, Mass.: Harvard University Press, Copyright, 1952, by the President and Fellows of Harvard College. Reprinted by permission of the publisher.

mentioned. The utility of that mood, some of its origins, and the way in which it unifies and makes effective the sonnet are worth analysis.

> That time of year thou mayst in me behold
> When yellow leaves, or none, or few, do hang
> Upon those boughs which shake against the cold,
> Bare ruin'd choirs, where late the sweet birds sang.
> In me thou see'st the twilight of such day
> As after sunset fadeth in the west,
> Which by and by black night doth take away,
> Death's second self, that seals up all in rest.
> In me thou see'st the glowing of such fire,
> That on the ashes of his youth doth lie,
> As the death-bed whereon it must expire
> Consum'd with that which it was nourish'd by.
>   This thou perceiv'st, which makes thy love more strong,
>   To love that well which thou must leave ere long.[1]

The quatrains here are clearly divided, the first devoting itself to an image of trees in early winter or late fall, the second to an image of twilight and the beginning of night, and the third to the image of a dying fire. The relationship of these to the professed subject of the poem, old age, is fairly obvious, and it might be said that the sonnet is merely an application of these images to the idea. However, Shakespeare's method is not quite so simple as this, and the way in which the images are worked out and the way in which they influence each other are worth notice.

The indirectness of Shakespeare's method could hardly better be exemplified than in the first quatrain. Here the picture of the trees in winter is used to project a situation of the feelings, rather than the external attributes of age. "When yellow leaves, or none, or few": the uncertainty here is clearly deliberate. Yellow leaves as a symbol of age are obvious enough, even if we do not recall Macbeth's "My way of life is fall'n into the sere, the yellow leaf," but the curious effect produced here is by the alternatives of "yellow leaves," "none," and "few." Then the purely descriptive part of the image is extended, with "upon those boughs which shake against the cold" carrying us farther into the picture of win-

[1] Brooke, *Shakespeare's Sonnets*, p. 163.

ter and away from the relationship between the speaker and
the image. If we stop at this point and ask of the first line,
In what respect may this time of year be seen "in me," there
is no answer, for the figure has left the speaker behind and
developed in a purely descriptive direction. But then in line
4 the boughs themselves are made the subject of further
metaphor, "bare ruin'd choirs," and then returned immedi-
ately to their first existence as boughs by the "explanation"
of the choir figure, "where late the sweet birds sang."

The problem here is one of deciding just what the nature
of this figure is. To what degree does the image of the speaker
remain in the reader's eye: are those boughs which shake
against the cold supposed to cause us to picture an old man's
arms? When the boughs are momentarily transformed by the
"bare ruin'd choirs," are we to evoke very fully the picture
of the decayed monastery churches with their ruined choirs
and, as William Empson suggests,[2] the choirboys themselves,
and associate this with the feeling of the poet toward the
young man addressed? The control of the associations is
very difficult. In general, it seems safest to say that the con-
nections between the picture, doubly metaphorical, of the
winter boughs is only atmospherically and symbolically con-
nected with "in me." There is nothing of an allegorical cor-
respondence or even a conceit. It is this reticence about the
application of the description to the subject that allows for
further development in the following quatrains.

The image of twilight fading and being taken away by
night brings the imagery closer to the subject, for the night
is called "Death's second self," and the ambiguous "that
seals up all in rest" applies to both night and death, the two
selves. "Seals up" is another of those rural terms common
in Shakespeare's figurative language; it applies to putting
cattle away for the night.[3]

The third quatrain uses the image of a dying fire, and here
there is a genuine conceit. The fire still burns, but on the

2 Seven Types of Ambiguity (London, 1930), p. 3.
3 See T. G. Tucker, The Sonnets of Shakespeare (Cambridge, England,
1924), p. 149. In some ways Tucker's edition is the most useful of all
editions of the sonnets, especially for the kind of analysis which I have
been attempting here. He is, however, insufficiently sensitive to ambiguities
in meaning, and his comment will often dogmatize on a single meaning
when two or more exist at once.

ashes of what has been already burnt. This is like old age, which rests on the youth which has produced it. But an additional idea is that this is a deathbed, relating our associations to the night–death image of the preceding quatrain, and the idea of a bed of ashes inevitably suggests repentance and humiliation. Moreover, the ashes tend to choke the fire, though they represent former fire, former fuel. Therefore, we get a formulation of a favorite idea of Shakespeare's: "Consum'd with that which it was nourish'd by." The irony of process, as it might be called, has many expressions in these sonnets; it is an indication of the antique cast of Shakespeare's mind: "And time that gave doth now his gift confound."[4]

Sonnet 73 is clear in its general design. The three quatrains have a relationship to each other and a natural development. They proceed from the declining of the year to the declining of the day to a declining of the fire, bringing the metaphorical point closer to the subject as the poem progresses. But the relationship of the figures to each other is also a metaphorical one: the year and the day are both metaphors for a lifetime; the fire has to do both with the heat and life of summer and noonday as well as with the vital essence of life. The richness of the sonnet derives more from its metaphorical involutions than it does from the clarity of its structure.[5]

4 Sonnet 60.
5 R. M. Alden (*The Sonnets of Shakespeare* [Boston, 1916], p. 183) called this "the finest example of the Shakespearian mode," presumably because of its structure, for Alden is so resistant to the metaphors in Shakespeare that he recoiled with horror at some of the more obvious images in sonnet 60, preferring to pretend that they are not there. John Crowe Ransom's essay, "Shakespeare at Sonnets," *Southern Review*, III (1937–38), 531–553, republished in *The World's Body* (New York, 1938), comments on and praises the three-quatrain sonnets above the others. Arthur Mizener's reply to Ransom in *Southern Review*, V (1939–40), 730–747, deals with the structure of Shakespeare's figurative language. The line in sonnet 73 which I discussed only briefly, "Bare ruin'd choirs, where late the sweet birds sang," offers an example of the difficulties of critics: Ransom says he deplores the coexistence of the images of the boughs shaking against the cold and of the bare ruin'd choirs; not only this but he also says, "I believe everybody will deprecate *sweet*" ("Shakespeare at Sonnets," p. 550). Tucker, on the other hand, does not deprecate it. He says, "The epithet is not idle; the choirs formerly rang with 'sweet' singing. The implication is 'I was a summer poet once'" (*The Sonnets of Shakespeare*, p. 149).

WINIFRED M. T. NOWOTTNY

Formal Elements in Shakespeare's Sonnets: Sonnets I–VI

Despite Shakespeare's own description of his sonnets as being "far from variation or quick change," they have proved to be remarkably resistant to generalizations. It is, however, the purpose of this article to suggest that there is one generalization that can be made about them; one, moreover, that affords a point of view from which it is always helpful to regard them: namely, that the *Sonnets* reveal Shakespeare's strong sense of form, and that it is with respect to their form that the peculiar features or striking effects of individual sonnets may best be understood. There are in the *Sonnets* so many experiments with form that it would be difficult to lay down at the outset a definition of "form" at once comprehensive and precise, but the meaning of the term as it is used here will be sufficiently indicated by describing "form" as "that in virtue of which the parts are related one to another," or indeed as "that which manifests itself in the relationships of the parts." What is important for the purposes of this article is not the precise definition of form, but rather the indication of elements which commonly contribute to the manifestation of form. At the present day, the most illuminating criticism

From *Essays in Criticism*, II (January 1952), pp. 76–84. Reprinted by permission of Basil Blackwell, publisher.

of individual sonnets is characterized by its concentration on imagery, and though it is true that imagery in the *Sonnets* is of great importance, it is not of exclusive or even of paramount importance. In this article I shall try to show that in Shakespeare's sonnets imagery is subordinated to the creation of the form of the whole and that imagery itself is at its most effective when it supports or is supported by the action of formal elements of a different kind.

Sonnets I–VI of the 1609 Quarto afford illustration. Shakespeare is often praised for his power of using imagery as an integrating element, yet in these sonnets it is evident that he has sacrificed the integration of the imagery of the individual sonnet to larger considerations of form; this sacrifice has features which show that it is in fact a sacrifice and not the ineptitude of a novice in sonnet-writing. In Sonnet I, the degree to which the images assist the organization of the poem is slight indeed. Almost every line has a separate image, and these images are heterogeneous (for instance: "Beauty's rose" — "heir" — "contracted" — "flame" — "famine" — "foe" — "herald" — "buriest" — "glutton"). The relation between the images is, for the most part, a relation via the subject they illustrate; it is not by their relations to one another that the poem is organized. This, however, is not ineptitude. The separateness, the repetitiveness (in that there is no increasing penetration of the object, but only an ever-renewed allegorization), and the regularity (a single new image in each of the first twelve lines) give this sonnet the character of a litany. If Sonnet I is indeed in its rightful place, there would seem to be here a recognizable decorum of form in the poet's electing to open by a litany of images[1] a sonnet sequence which makes extended use of each. Further, the hypothesis that in Sonnet I there is a decorum of form which to the poet seemed more important than the congruity of images within the individual sonnet is borne out by some features of Sonnets II–IV. The imagery of Sonnet II falls into two distinct parts connected by a modulation. In the first

[1] The litany of images is at the same time a litany of considerations or arguments, for in these sonnets the image is often an emblem of an argument.

quatrain there is a group of images all referring to the
beauty of the face; in the third quatrain a very different
group, not visual like the first, but moral or prudential, re-
lating to beauty considered as treasure, inheritance, and
a matter for the rendering of accounts; the intervening
quatrain is entirely devoted to a modulation from one type
to the other:

> Then, being ask'd where all thy beauty lies,
> Where all the treasure of thy lusty days,
> To say, within thine own deep-sunken eyes,
> Were an all-eating shame and thriftless praise.

(In this modulation the visual and the prudential—"beauty"
and "treasure"—are formally balanced, and the "deep-
sunken" unites the eyes and the treasure in a single imaging
epithet.) This careful four-line modulation suggests that
Shakespeare was well aware of the virtue of relating images
one to another as well as to the object they convey; yet the
very necessity for a modulation here derives from the re-
moteness from one another of the two types of imagery.
Here again the discrepancy finds its justification in larger
considerations of form: namely, in the relation of Sonnet II
to Sonnets III and IV. Sonnet III takes up and expands
the first quatrain of Sonnet II, turning as it does upon the
beauty of the face ("Look in thy glass, and tell the face
thou viewest . . ."), and Sonnet IV takes up and expands
the third quatrain of Sonnet II, turning as it does entirely
upon beauty as treasure, inheritance, and a matter for the
rendering of accounts. It is further to be observed that
Sonnets V and VI repeat this pattern, V dealing with visual
beauty in visual terms, and VI dealing with "beauty's
treasure" in a long-sustained conceit drawn from usury.
Would it be fanciful to suggest that the infelicity of the
usury conceit in Sonnet VI reflects the difficulty the poet
found in bringing this little sequence to a formally sym-
metrical conclusion?

In each of these six sonnets, features of the individual
sonnet are illuminated by a consideration of the design of
the whole group. But since we have no external warrant

of the correctness of the 1609 order, the case for Shakespeare's sense of form must further be argued on grounds affording independent corroboration. This is found in Sonnet IV where, though the imagery chosen relates the sonnet to its fellows, the development of that imagery within the sonnet is a self-contained exercise in abstract form. The sonnet must be quoted and discussed in full.

> Unthrifty loveliness, why dost thou spend
> Upon thyself thy beauty's legacy?
> Nature's bequest gives nothing, but doth lend,
> And, being frank, she lends to those are free.
> Then, beauteous niggard, why dost thou abuse
> The bounteous largess given thee to give?
> Profitless usurer, why dost thou use
> So great a sum of sums, yet canst not live?
> For, having traffic with thyself alone,
> Thou of thyself thy sweet self dost deceive.
> Then how when nature calls thee to be gone?
> What acceptable audit canst thou leave?
> > Thy unus'd beauty must be tomb'd with thee,
> > Which, used, lives, th'executor to be.

Here we have a sonnet in which, patently, there is a high degree of organization. Firstly, the imagery of financial matters is sustained throughout. Secondly, there is within this integrated scheme a number of strongly marked subsidiary systems. The most immediately striking, which may therefore be cited first, is the ringing of the changes in lines 5–8 on "abuse"—"usurer"—"use," which is taken up in the couplet by "unus'd," "used." Another marked system is that of the reflexive constructions associated with "thee": "spend upon thyself"—"traffic with thyself"— "thou of thyself thy sweet self dost deceive," taken up in the couplet by "thy . . . beauty . . . tomb'd with thee." That these are deliberate systems, not inept repetitions, is proved by the way in which they interlock in the couplet: "unus'd" is, in the first line of the couplet, linked with "thy beauty . . . tomb'd with thee," and this contrasts with the second line of the couplet, where there is a linking of "used," "executor," and "lives," to produce the complete formal balance in thought, diction and syntax, of

> Thy unus'd beauty must be tomb'd with thee,
> Which, used, lives, th'executor to be.

This formal balance is of course closely related to the thought of the sonnet: Nature, which lends beauty in order that it may be given, is contrasted with the youth, whose self-regarding results in a usurious living on capital alone, which is a negation of Nature and of life; these paradoxes of the thought make possible the correspondences and contrasts of the verbal systems. What is remarkable is the way in which the poet evolves from this material an intricate and beautiful form which is very close to the art of fugue. Like the fugue, its effect resides in the interaction of the parts; critical analysis, which cannot reproduce the simultaneousness of the original, must labor heavily behind, discussing first the development of each part and then their interaction. We may note, then, that "Unthrifty loveliness," with which the sonnet opens, is, as it were, a first blending of those two distinct voices, "why dost thou spend upon thyself" and "Nature's bequest." The second quatrain blends them again in "beauteous niggard," which is itself an inversion, formally complete, of "unthrifty loveliness," and moreover an inversion which leads on to the extreme of "profitless usurer"; further, the movement toward the judgment represented by "profitless usurer" has all the while been less obtrusively going on in the verbs as well as in the vocatives ("spend"—"abuse"—"yet canst not live"). Then, with "yet canst not live," the sonnet brings out the second voice, that reflexive (and self-destructive) action announced in "spend upon thyself," but kept low in the first eight lines, maintaining itself there only by the formal parallels of "why dost thou spend"—"why dost thou abuse"—"why dost thou use." This voice now emerges predominant in "For, having traffic with thyself alone," and this voice in turn reaches its extreme of formal development in the line "Thou of thyself thy sweet self dost deceive." The remaining lines bring the two voices to a sharp contrast with "nature calls thee to be gone" (where "nature" and "thee" achieve a syntactical nearness embodying a conflict of opposed concepts, and this conflict-in-nearness is fully stated in the complete formal balance of the couplet). In this rough analysis of the blending of the voices in this sonnet, much has had to be passed over, but now we may go back and point to the incidental contrast and harmony of "beauteous niggard" with "bounteous largess"; to the transition, in the pun of "canst not live," from usury to death (which leads on to the contrast in the couplet); to the felicity of "audit" in line 12, which is relevant not only to all the financial imagery that has gone before, but also to the rendering of an account when life is at an end; to the subtle conceptual sequence of "unthrifty loveliness" (the fact of beauty), "beauteous niggard" (the poet's reproof), "profitless usurer" (the youth's own loss), and finally, "unus'd beauty" (the whole tragedy—of beauty, of the poet, and of the youth—in the hour of death). Thus this sonnet, which in its absence of visual imagery has little attraction for the hasty reader, reveals itself to analysis as having an intricate beauty of form to which it would be hard to find a parallel in the work of any other poet.

Though Sonnet IV is a *tour de force* in the handling of form, Sonnet V is even more important to the critic who would make much of formal elements, in that it has a quality which sets it apart from the preceding four: a quality the average reader might call seriousness or sincerity. Here Shakespeare deals with Time and Beauty (and for the application of these to the particular case of the youth requires Sonnet VI, linked to V by "Then let not . . ."). The evident artifice of Sonnets I–IV (emblematic imagery, conceits, punning and patterned word play) gives place in Sonnet V to language which, though it is of course figurative, derives its figures from that realm of common experience in which processes conceived philosophically by the mind have in fact their manifestations to the senses: from the seasons which figure Time, from the flower and its fragrance which figure Beauty and Evanescence. In short, the poem appeals to us in that realm of experience where we are all, already, half poets. Yet despite this change from the "artificial" to the "sincere," this poem too derives much of its strength from its formal design. This design is simple but perfect. The easy continuous process of Time is stated in lines themselves easy and continuous:

> Those hours that with gentle work did frame
> The lovely gaze where every eye doth dwell,

and in the next two lines, which suggest that this process implies a coming reversal, the reversal is still a thing of the future and is indicated not by any change in the movement but only by the verbal contrasts between "gentle" and "will play the tyrant" and between "fairly" and "unfair." So the continuous movement flows uninterrupted through these lines and on into the fifth:

> For never-resting time leads summer on

but in the sixth line,

> To hideous winter and confounds him there

the reversal so casually foretold in the first quatrain becomes, by the violence of "hideous winter" and "confounds" and by the change of tense, a present catastrophe, and the movement of the fifth and sixth lines taken together perfectly corresponds to the sense: the running-on movement of summer is checked by "hideous winter" and again by the heavy pause at "there." The next two lines embody perfectly, by sound and imagery as well as by sense, this checking and reversal:

> Sap check'd with frost and lusty leaves quite gone,
> Beauty o'ersnow'd and bareness everywhere.

(Particularly subtle is the way in which the alliteration of "lusty leaves" gives place to that of "beauty" with "bareness.") Now in the remaining six lines the poet in his turn attempts a reversal, and the beauty of the form is to be seen in the way in which he now uses the two kinds of movement already laid down in the sonnet (the one of flowing, the other of checking). What he does is to *transfer to Beauty* the flowing movement of Time, and then to *arrest* Beauty in a state of permanent *perfection;* this he does by the long flowing movement, ending in arrest and permanence, of the line,

> Then, were not summer's distillation left . . .

This triumphant transfer to Beauty of the movement formerly associated with Time, is of a piece with the imagery of the next line ("A liquid prisoner pent in walls of glass"), where Beauty's distillation is at once arrested ("prisoner," "pent") yet free ("liquid") and visible ("glass"); this image of course reverses the implications of the earlier images of winter, where the sap was checked with frost and beauty was o'ersnow'd. Thus the movement of the first eight lines proves to have been designed not merely to make the sound repeat the sense, but rather to lay down formal elements whose reversal enables the poet to reverse the reversal implicit in Time. Similarly, the image of distillation is seen to be not merely an illustration of the concept of preserving Beauty, but also an answer to the image of winter's freezing of the sap and obliteration of Beauty. Clearly, the formal elements of Sonnet V are part of the poetic logic: the movement, as much as the imagery, is a means of poetic power. It is because of this that the study of formal elements in the *Sonnets* is not an arid academic exercise. Such a study can help one to arrive at a fuller understanding of Shakespeare's means of communication and a fuller possession of those poetic experiences with which the *Sonnets* deal.

This article has dealt only with the first six sonnets of the 1609 Quarto. These six sonnets are not exceptional in their successful handling of form; from the whole range of the *Sonnets* many examples more subtle and more striking might have been chosen but it seemed to me best, in order to argue the case for Shakespeare's interest in form, to make no arbitrary selection, but simply to begin at the beginning and scrutinize what is to be found there. The findings warrant a much greater attention to formal aspects of the *Sonnets* than is at present customary. The result of such an attentiveness to Shakespeare's handling of form is the discovery that the greater the immediate effect of a sonnet, the more surely does it prove, upon examination, that the effects rest no less upon the form than upon the appeal of the sentiments or of the imagery (as, for instance, in the famous Sonnet CXVI, "Let me not to the marriage of true minds . . ."). Again, it will be found that many of the

sonnets which are not commonly held to be of the finest,
reveal an unsuspected depth and strength when they are,
after scrutiny of their form, revalued. It is upon this last
point that particular stress may well be laid, for it is here
that one becomes aware of new possibilities for the inter-
pretation of Shakespeare's language, not only in the poems
but also in the plays. A close study of the language of the
Sonnets makes it clear that, great as was Shakespeare's
ability to use imagery not only for its beauty but also for
its integrating power, he possessed in even greater measure
the power to make the formal elements of language express
the nature of the experience with which the language deals.
No doubt a knowledge of rhetoric, which must direct atten-
tion to verbal patterns, did something to develop this power.
Of the early plays it may be true to say that sometimes the
rhetorical forms are empty, that they have little virtue be-
yond that of providing a ready-made mold for the flow of
what is thought and felt. But Shakespeare's rejection of
rhetorical forms of the overelaborate and merely self-
regarding type was coupled with an increasing awareness
of the expressiveness of those forms he did retain. Thus in
the language of the great plays the recurrence of a marked
form is not fortuitous, nor is it, in cases where a recurring
form is associated with a particular speaker, merely a de-
vice for adding body to a character; that is to say, these
features of the style are rarely, if ever, designed to con-
tribute merely to the creation of a "character part"; they
are almost always an expression of something essential in
the speaker himself considered in his relation to the play
as a whole. Pope in his preface to his edition of Shake-
speare commented on the highly individualized styles of
the characters. It still remains for the interpreters of
Shakespeare in our own time to discover to what extent
these styles are expressive as well as characteristic. And
further it may be said that the expressiveness of formal
organizations in Shakespeare's language is matched by the
expressiveness of form in all his dramatic structures. Every
age rediscovers the genius of Shakespeare. It is open to
ours to discover and to show the working of his genius in
the realm of forms.

HELEN VENDLER

Shakespeare's Sonnets: The Uses of Synecdoche

In his sonnets, Shakespeare takes up very large themes —love, jealousy, death. We could say that the very first aesthetic problem such themes present is their unmanageability. Unless they can be reduced to manageable size, the poet cannot create a believable poem. In finding an almost infinite variety of manageable structures, Shakespeare exercised his best ingenuity; and the example of success in this mode that I want to take up here is an apparently playful sonnet depending on synecdoche, the trope *par excellence* of reduction, which usually takes the form of substituting the part for the whole, for example "roof" for "house," or "hands" for "workers." The sonnet finds in synecdoche a solution to the aesthetic problem of how one represents sexual jealousy in other than tragic or satiric terms. By understanding that a problem is being solved, we can understand the aesthetic gaiety of the comic solution, and we end by conceiving of this sonnet not as a frigid triviality (as the more solemn commentators would have it) but rather as a triumphant *jeu d'esprit* on the dangerous subject of sexual infidelity.

The sonnet I take up is #128:

This essay has been written especially for the Signet edition of Shakespeare's *Sonnets*.

How oft, when thou my music music play'st
Upon that blessèd wood whose motion sounds
With thy sweet fingers when thou gently sway'st
The wiry concord that mine ear confounds,
Do I envy those jacks that nimble leap
To kiss the tender inward of thy hand,
Whilst my poor lips, which should that harvest reap,
At the wood's boldness by thee blushing stand.
To be so tickled they would change their state
And situation with those dancing chips,
O'er whom thy fingers walk with gentle gait,
Making dead wood more blest than living lips.
     Since saucy jacks so happy are in this,
     Give them thy fingers, me thy lips to kiss.

We recall Romeo's wish that he could be a glove upon
the hand of Juliet so that he might touch her cheek. Here,
the speaker's wish to be a musical "jack" or key touched
by his mistress's hand, is not taken literally, any more than
Romeo's wish to be a glove. Readers can become impa-
tient with such a conceit (a figurative expression); they
feel they are being asked to concur in language inappro-
priate to a grown man. But in fact there is no such "real"
wish; the object in the conceit serves as a miniature surro-
gate actor playing on an invented stage the drama of
physical touch that the lover wishes to act out in "real
life." The absurdity of the drama of reduction (in which a
glove or keyboard plays the role desired by the lover)
lends the fantasy its aesthetic interest. Shakespeare pro-
longs his conceit for fourteen lines, and uses it to deflect
feelings of sexual competition too painful for direct
utterance.

When Shakespeare's playlet opens, the lover is standing
by his mistress as she plays the virginals, wishing that he
could be the "blessèd wood" that resounds under the
touch of her "sweet fingers." The conceit of the poem is
apparently so brief—"I envy the wood that kisses your
hand"—that one principal aesthetic project here must
simply be to keep invention going. In the first quatrain,

only tender words are addressed to the mistress. She is herself her lover's music, her fingers are sweet, her playing gentle, and her touch a blessing. Scarcely a line passes without the interjection of some melting word of praise. (In fact, the whole poem, before the couplet, is bracketed by the two words "blest" and "gentle": the "blessèd wood" becomes "wood more blest," and the concord "gently" swayed engenders the "gentle" gait near the close.)

To reinforce the apparent semantic tenderness, a mimic conjunction of lover and lady is played out in the poem by antiphonal pronominal kisses—my music, thy fingers; mine ear, thy hand; my lips, thy fingers; thy fingers, me, thy lips—thereby exhibiting the private, but frustrated, desire for union which has engendered the speaker's mock jealousy of the instrument's "saucy jacks." The bracketing of the drama early and late by "blest" and "gentle" and "fingers" tells us that the fictional situation does not change between lines one and twelve: the wood is still *blest* because of the continued *gentle* playing of the lady's *fingers* upon it. The central project of invention, then, is to modify, during twelve lines, the lover's response to an unchanging situation. It is a project so fragile that too heavy a hand will wreck it.

Shakespeare schematizes the scene, as I have said, by reduction through synecdoche. He reduces the lady, seated, into a hand and fingers; he reduces the lover, standing beside her, into an eye, an ear, and lips. The courting-concert has been a rich subject for genre-paintings; if we think of the amount of decorative incident possible given a room, a lady, a gentleman, and a musical instrument, we become keenly aware of Shakespeare's drastic reduction of the scene to bodily synecdoche. At first, as I have said, the speaker is an ear, an implied eye watching the lady, a self referred to as "I," and a pair of lips; his ear, he tells us, is confounded, his eye watches the nimble jacks as they leap, he envies the wood, and his lips blush at the wood's boldness. The first eight lines of the sonnet are a sketch, then, in which a complex human scene is reduced to its very few active elements. We might conceive of such a poem as a drawing in which an image has been reduced to the minimum number of barely descriptive strokes.

But there is even a reduction of this reduction. In the third quatrain the lover is further reduced to nothing but a pair of lips, the lady to nothing but a set of fingers. Here, the lover also abandons the first person, and speaks of his lips in the third person, thereby affecting an impartial "outside" judgment on her fingers and his lips alike. This third-quatrain narrowing and reconceiving of the conceit, done of course in the service of erotic argument (so that the lover and the lady can equally be spectators of the poor disenfranchised lips) turns the poem from present-time habitual retrospect ("How oft") to conditional-mood hopeful prospect ("To be so tickled, [my lips] would change their state / And situation with those dancing chips").

Finally, in the couplet, the continuing synecdoche for the lady (her fingers) is suddenly and winningly changed to an element (lips) that the lover has already been said to own, but which the lady has not yet been mentioned as possessing. And the lover (who in the couplet resumes his first-person account) has so recently been represented by his lips alone that the plea "Give . . . me thy lips" is itself, by the conjunction of "me" and "thy lips," that desired kiss of lips to lips toward which the poem has been aspiring and on which it ends. The poem is a kiss deferred and, finally, a kiss verbally enacted; one aesthetic problem of the sonnet is that of finding a way to enact the lover's yearning to kiss, and its final implied success.

I have neglected till now the introductory metaphor of the sonnet, the metaphor of music. The tonic note is sounded in the opening sigh, "How oft, when thou my music music play'st." The rest of the poem exists to amplify the sense in which, by synecdoche, the lady can be called the lover's music. What is emphasized about music here is the erotic reciprocity between player and instrument (one of the countless images of reciprocity in the sonnets, reciprocity being one of their directing metaphors). This reciprocity at first opposes a conventional female gentleness to an equally conventional male bold leap to kiss; but it later adds, we should notice, a female provocative tickling and a male responsive dancing, suggesting the lady's deliberate unchastity. "Music" as we see it here is an affair of a body that both initiates and responds, offering concord and confusion at once.

In the throes of his mock jealousy of the jacks, the lover will refer self-deprecatingly to "my poor lips"; but as he prepares to argue his own case, he calls the jacks "dead wood," while he, by contrast, possesses "living lips." Until this moment, he had ostensibly hoped only that the lady's *fingers* might stray away from the nimble jacks and toward his lips; but now his mock envy turns to a mock largesse, as he invents a more fitting cessation to the drama. Let the music continue, he suggests, thereby satisfying the jacks and granting the lady her desire to continue "tickling" them; but let a kiss be offered in the lover's direction: "Since saucy jacks so happy are in this, / Give them thy fingers, me thy lips to kiss." The jacks are allocated the fingers as their portion (in the quarto, the line reads "give them their fingers"); to the lover are allocated the surprising lips (which until this moment the lady did not verbally possess). The distribution of benefits is announced, it would seem, with a happiness which is delighted that all concerned can be satisfied at once.

But behind the mock envy, the mock largesse, and the animated fiction of the jacks that leap across the line break to kiss; behind the self-deprecation of mock modesty as the timid lover stands blushing at the sexual audacity of the jacks, there lies the recollection—ironic of course but touching—of the hyperbolic treasuring in adolescence of all proximity to the beloved. Doting is an emotion not much described in verse: adults are ashamed to dote. But this is a poem content to be abject in doting —longing to blush, to be tickled, to dance, to kiss, to worship every motion of the beloved, even at the price of sharing her with other lovers.

The metamorphosis proposed by the lover—that his lips should themselves change state and situation and become dancing chips in order to receive the favors of the lady—never has to take place, but it serves to enact the hopeless intensities of sexual jealousy on a comically reduced plane. The jacks reap the harvest that rightfully belongs to the lover. The lady shows no disposition to give up the kisses of the jacks—on the contrary, she deliberately tickles the jacks into their responsive leaps. The first thirteen lines of the poem are, we realize at the end, an elaborate pretext to justify the prayer of the fourteenth; and the fourteenth rings as conclusively as it does because it is a phonetic re-inscription. It inscribes over "leap / To kiss" (the action of the jacks) the homonymic phrase "lips to kiss" (the hope of the lover).

In Shakespeare's reduction, the erogenous zones (including here the ear and the fingers, as well as the palm and the lips) eventually take on such importance that the other parts of the body, and all surrounding items, pale into insignificance. In the final totalization of the original synecdoche, she is all fingers and lips, he entirely a yearning pair of living lips. And only one action is permitted to exist—the touch of one element to another, the kiss of fingers to wood, or lips to lips.

The problem of conveying, in a comic mode, the eroticized and tormented state of the sensibility of the lover has been solved both economically and elegantly, with a leavening of bitter humor that permits sexual suggestiveness while aestheticizing it in the convention of courtship by music. The terrors of infidelity, jealousy, promiscuity, and sexual mistress-sharing are brought down to manageable proportions. Shakespeare's brilliant verbal solution has the tact to remain at the playful level of the set problem—the "correct" distribution of the lady's erotic energies. The final verbal kiss satisfies both the lady's free will (she can still give her fingers to the jacks) and the lover's yearning.

It is probably no accident that this displacement of jealousy into comedy is followed, in sonnets 129 (on lust) and 131 (on the lady's "black" deeds), by the furious return of the repressed.

The usefulness of the figure of synecdoche lies not only in its reducing to manageability the agonies of love. It lies as well in what this trope manages to exclude. Fixing, as it does, on one or two elements—here, fingers and lips— it succeeds in excluding the whole world of other objects, competing essences. It suggests, in miniature, what the aesthetic of the sonnet sequence itself must be, as it reduces the world to a very few personages—the lover, his beloved, his rivals. To those accustomed to the wide social sweep of fiction this reduction may seem a defect. But it is a mistake to think of the lyric as acting in a world smaller than that of other literary fictions. On the contrary, it acts in the only world there is—the world extending vertically from the Trinity (105) to hell (129), and horizontally from East to West (132). Lyric enlarges its personae to fill that cosmic space: the personages in lyric are so great that the world can contain only two or three of them at once. They usurp all available space. The speaker says of his love that it fears not policy, "but all alone stands hugely politic" (124). Shakespeare's need to reduce suggests the anterior daunting immensity of his theme; his frequent turn from reduction to hyperbole implies that the innate grandeur of love will make itself felt, even when reduced to a set of eyes, lips, or fingers. What is implicit, in this raising of the human figure to the scale of all that exists, is the vastness, to human consideration, of the self and its immediate concerns.

The sonnet sequence asserts that human relations are worthy of an (almost) infinite number of poems devoted to aspects of love. We can draw a parallel between the value Shakespeare accords to love and the value he accords to the sonnet form: the form cannot be exhausted, any more than its topic can. In the sequence, the sonnet form tirelessly re-inscribes itself as if in scorn of all other lyric forms; the topic of love re-inscribes itself as if in scorn of any other interest proffered by the larger world. The sonnets, in their exploration, ever deeper and deeper, of a single poetic form and a single topic, suggest that the centripetal aspect of consciousness cannot be adequately embodied in the linearity of the novel or the dialectic of drama, but can find itself only in a poetry of lyric intensity, in which a single sensibility sounds the expressive potential of a single topic in the ultimate service of the depth of our inner life.

Shakespeare's use of consciously maintained tropes suggests his sustained interest in the fictions of the mind. We see in the sonnets his continued analysis of the power of the mind to greatly restrict or greatly expand the scale of its perceptions, to change its opinions, to clarify the obscure by reinspection, to fantasize, to adjust its fictions to an uncooperative reality, to luxuriate in its own inventions, and above all—as he writes his argument of love— to deepen its investigations of a profound idea while deepening at the same time its power over a flexible and inexhaustible poetic form.

Suggested References

The number of possible references is vast and grows alarmingly. (The *Shakespeare Quarterly* devotes one issue each year to a list of the previous year's work, and *Shakespeare Survey* —an annual publication—includes a substantial review of recent scholarship, as well as an occasional essay surveying a few decades of scholarship on a chosen topic.) Though no works are indispensable, those listed below have been found helpful.

1. Shakespeare's Times

Byrne, M. St. Clare. *Elizabethan Life in Town and Country*. Rev. ed. New York: Barnes & Noble, 1961. Chapters on manners, beliefs, education, etc., with illustrations.

Joseph, B. L. *Shakespeare's Eden: The Commonwealth of England, 1558–1629*. New York: Barnes & Noble, 1971. An account of the social, political, economic, and cultural life of England.

Schoenbaum, S. *Shakespeare: The Globe and the World*. New York: Oxford University Press, 1979. A readable, handsomely illustrated book on the world of the Elizabethans.

Shakespeare's England. 2 vols. London: Oxford University Press, 1916. A large collection of scholarly essays on a wide variety of topics (e.g. astrology, costume, gardening, horsemanship), with special attention to Shakespeare's references to these topics.

Stone, Lawrence. *The Crisis of the Aristocracy, 1558–1641*, abridged edition. London: Oxford University Press, 1967.

2. Shakespeare

Barnet, Sylvan. *A Short Guide to Shakespeare*. New York: Harcourt Brace Jovanovich, 1974. An introduction to all of the works and to the dramatic traditions behind them.

Bentley, Gerald E. *Shakespeare: A Biographical Handbook.*

New Haven, Conn.: Yale University Press, 1961. The facts about Shakespeare, with virtually no conjecture intermingled.

Bush, Geoffrey. *Shakespeare and the Natural Condition.* Cambridge, Mass.: Harvard University Press, 1956. A short, sensitive account of Shakespeare's view of "Nature," touching most of the works.

Chambers, E. K. *William Shakespeare: A Study of Facts and Problems.* 2 vols. London: Oxford University Press, 1930. An invaluable, detailed reference work; not for the casual reader.

Chute, Marchette. *Shakespeare of London.* New York: Dutton, 1949. A readable biography fused with portraits of Stratford and London life.

Clemen, Wolfgang H. *The Development of Shakespeare's Imagery.* Cambridge, Mass.: Harvard University Press, 1951. (Originally published in German, 1936.) A temperate account of a subject often abused.

Granville-Barker, Harley. *Prefaces to Shakespeare.* 2 vols. Princeton, N.J.: Princeton University Press, 1946–47. Essays on ten plays by a scholarly man of the theater.

Harbage, Alfred. *As They Liked It.* New York: Macmillan, 1947. A long, sensitive essay on Shakespeare, morality, and the audience's expectations.

Kernan, Alvin B., ed. *Modern Shakespearean Criticism: Essays on Style, Dramaturgy, and the Major Plays.* New York: Harcourt Brace Jovanovich, 1970. A collection of major formalist criticism.

———. "The Plays and the Playwrights." In *The Revels History of Drama in English,* general editors Clifford Leech and T. W. Craik. Vol. III. London: Methuen, 1975. A book-length essay surveying Elizabethan drama with substantial discussions of Shakespeare's plays.

Schoenbaum, S. *Shakespeare's Lives.* Oxford: Clarendon Press, 1970. A review of the evidence, and an examination of many biographies, including those by Baconians and other heretics.

———. *William Shakespeare: A Compact Documentary Life.* New York: Oxford University Press, 1977. A readable presentation of all that the documents tell us about Shakespeare.

Traversi, D. A. *An Approach to Shakespeare.* 3rd rev. ed. 2 vols. New York: Doubleday, 1968–69. An analysis of the plays beginning with words, images, and themes, rather than with characters.

Van Doren, Mark. *Shakespeare*. New York: Holt, 1939. Brief, perceptive readings of all of the plays.

3. Shakespeare's Theater

Beckerman, Bernard. *Shakespeare at the Globe, 1599–1609*. New York: Macmillan, 1962. On the playhouse and on Elizabethan dramaturgy, acting, and staging.

Chambers, E. K. *The Elizabethan Stage*. 4 vols. New York: Oxford University Press, 1945. A major reference work on theaters, theatrical companies, and staging at court.

Cook, Ann Jennalie. *The Privileged Playgoers of Shakespeare's London, 1576–1642*. Princeton, N.J.: Princeton University Press, 1981. Sees Shakespeare's audience as more middle-class and more intellectual than Harbage (below) does.

Gurr, Andrew. *The Shakespearean Stage: 1579–1642*. 2nd edition. Cambridge: Cambridge University Press, 1980. On the acting companies, the actors, the playhouses, the stages, and the audiences.

Harbage, Alfred. *Shakespeare's Audience*. New York: Columbia University Press, 1941. A study of the size and nature of the theatrical public, emphasizing its representativeness.

Hodges, C. Walter. *The Globe Restored*. London: Ernest Benn, 1953; New York: Coward-McCann, Inc., 1954. A well-illustrated and readable attempt to reconstruct the Globe Theatre.

Hosley, Richard. "The Playhouses." In *The Revels History of Drama in English*, general editors Clifford Leech and T. W. Craik. Vol. III. London: Methuen, 1975. An essay of one hundred pages on the physical aspects of the playhouses.

Kernodle, George R. *From Art to Theatre: Form and Convention in the Renaissance*. Chicago: University of Chicago Press, 1944. Pioneering and stimulating work on the symbolic and cultural meanings of theater construction.

Nagler, A. M. *Shakespeare's Stage*. Trans. Ralph Manheim. New Haven, Conn.: Yale University Press, 1958. A very brief introduction to the physical aspects of the playhouse.

Slater, Ann Pasternak. *Shakespeare the Director*. Totowa, N.J.: Barnes & Noble, 1982. An analysis of theatrical effects (e.g., kissing, kneeling) in stage directions and dialogue.

Thomson, Peter. *Shakespeare's Theatre*. London: Routledge and Kegan Paul, 1983. A discussion of how plays were staged in Shakespeare's time.

4. Miscellaneous Reference Works

Abbott, E. A. *A Shakespearean Grammar*. New edition. New York: Macmillan, 1877. An examination of differences between Elizabethan and modern grammar.

Bevington, David. *Shakespeare*. Arlington Heights, Ill.: A. H. M. Publishing, 1978. A short guide to hundreds of important writings on the works.

Bullough, Geoffrey. *Narrative and Dramatic Sources of Shakespeare*. 8 vols. New York: Columbia University Press, 1957–75. A collection of many of the books Shakespeare drew upon, with judicious comments.

Campbell, Oscar James, and Edward G. Quinn. *The Reader's Encyclopedia of Shakespeare*. New York: Crowell, 1966. More than 2,600 entries, from a few sentences to a few pages, on everything related to Shakespeare.

Greg, W. W. *The Shakespeare First Folio*. New York: Oxford University Press, 1955. A detailed yet readable history of the first collection (1623) of Shakespeare's plays.

Kökeritz, Helge. *Shakespeare's Names*. New Haven, Conn.: Yale University Press, 1959. A guide to the pronunciation of some 1,800 names appearing in Shakespeare.

————. *Shakespeare's Pronunciation*. New Haven, Conn.: Yale University Press, 1953. Contains much information about puns and rhymes.

Muir, Kenneth. *The Sources of Shakespeare's Plays*. New Haven, Conn.: Yale University Press, 1978. An account of Shakespeare's use of his reading.

The Norton Facsimile: The First Folio of Shakespeare. Prepared by Charlton Hinman. New York: Norton, 1968. A handsome and accurate facsimile of the first collection (1623) of Shakespeare's plays.

Onions, C. T. *A Shakespeare Glossary*. 2nd ed., rev., with enlarged addenda. London: Oxford University Press, 1953. Definitions of words (or senses of words) now obsolete.

Partridge, Eric. *Shakespeare's Bawdy*. Rev. ed. New York: Dutton; London: Routledge & Kegan, 1955. A glossary of bawdy words and phrases.

Shakespeare Quarterly. See headnote to Suggested References.

Shakespeare Survey. See headnote to Suggested References.

Shakespeare's Plays in Quarto. A Facsimile Edition. Ed. Michael J. B. Allen and Kenneth Muir. Berkeley, Calif.: University of California Press, 1981. A book of nine hundred pages, containing facsimiles of twenty-two of the quarto editions of Shakespeare's plays. An invaluable complement to *The Norton Facsimile: The First Folio of Shakespeare* (see above).

Smith, Gordon Ross. *A Classified Shakespeare Bibliography 1936–1958.* University Park, Pa.: Pennsylvania State University Press, 1963. A list of some twenty thousand items on Shakespeare.

Spevack, Marvin. *The Harvard Concordance to Shakespeare.* Cambridge, Mass.: Harvard University Press, 1973. An index to Shakespeare's words.

Wells, Stanley, ed. *Shakespeare: Select Bibliographies.* London: Oxford University Press, 1973. Seventeen essays surveying scholarship and criticism of Shakespeare's life, work, and theater.

5. The Sonnets

Booth, Stephen. *An Essay on Shakespeare's Sonnets.* New Haven: Yale University Press, 1969.

Dubrow, Heather. *Captive Visitors: Shakespeare's Narrative Poems and Sonnets.* Ithaca: Cornell University Press, 1987.

Ferry, Anne Davidson. *The "Inward" Language: Sonnets of Wyatt, Sidney, Shakespeare, Donne.* Chicago: University of Chicago Press, 1983.

Fineman, Joel. *Shakespeare's Perjured Eye: The Invention of Poetic Subjectivity in the Sonnets.* Berkeley: University of California Press, 1985.

Hubler, Edward, and Northrop Frye, Leslie A. Fiedler, Stephen Spender, and R. P. Blackmur. *The Riddle of Shakespeare's Sonnets.* New York: Basic Books, 1962.

Ingram, W. G., and Theodore Redpath, eds. *Shakespeare's Sonnets.* 3rd impression. London: Hodder and Stoughton, 1978.

Kerrigan, John, ed. *The Sonnets and A Lover's Complaint.* New York: Viking, 1986.

Landry, Hilton. *Interpretations in Shakespeare's Sonnets.* Berkeley: University of California Press, 1963.

Leishman, J. B. *Themes and Variations in Shakespeare's Sonnets.* New York: Hillary House, 1962.

Melchiori, Giorgio. *Shakespeare's Dramatic Meditations.* Oxford: Clarendon Press, 1976.

Muir, Kenneth. *Shakespeare's Sonnets.* London: Allen & Unwin, 1979.

Nicoll, Allardyce, ed. *Shakespeare Survey 15.* Cambridge: Cambridge University Press, 1962.

Rollins, Hyder Edward, ed. *The Sonnets.* 2 vols. Philadelphia: Lippincott, 1944.

Index of First Lines

MENTOR Books of Plays